The End of the World… Again
Or
Hitbodedut

Book Zero, The Prequel

J. M. Dark

Credits to:

My wife Linda for putting up with me

and Enya for putting me in the mood

Tangar pulled his hair back and cinched a band of cloth around his forehead. "They must be important."

Stafon sat next to him on the fallen tree they had decided to use as a rest stop. "Important to whom? I mean, you saw them… It's just a pile of old rags."

Talbot remained standing in favor of the shade provided by a nearby tree. "Nolan for one."

Tangar dug into his pack for the snack he had brought. "Nolan is an old fool. He spends all his time kissing up to those tea drinkers on the council."

Talbot took the strip of dried meat offered. "Careful now... Nolan is Bishain's favorite. He tends to the council's fondness for spirit-tea to gain special privileges from the chosen few."

Tangar offered the snack to Stafon. "Oh, you don't know that. That's just jealous rumors. Besides, if they're just meaningless old rags, why do they keep them hidden away like that?"

Talbot tugged at the meat. "I don't know. It makes them seem more important that way. I mean, no one has cared about them for generations. Why are they suddenly important now?"

Stafon passed on the snack as he used the butt of his spear to wedge a small rock loose, sending it careening down the cliff and into the ocean below. "I guess it doesn't really matter. Nolan's going to test us on them whether they're important or not."

Tangar stuffed the remaining meat back into his pack. "Yeah... But, why all the secrecy? I mean, he pulled us aside like it was some kind of great revelation that others aren't worthy of, and he just lets us peek at them, like they're going to bite or something."

Talbot joined Stafon in dislodging rocks from the cliff. "They're part of the 'old-ways'. He said that Bishain has chosen us to care for the wisdom of the Shanare and that we're not to tell any of the 'enlightened-few'. It's some kind of honor or something."

Tangar rose from the log and pulled his pack over his shoulder. "Honor – what good is an honor if no one knows of it? Come on you guys; let's go before you cause this whole cliff to fall in with us on it."

The Gathering

The annual gathering of the tribes continued through the worst part of the winter months. The gathering village nestled on a broad plain spreading up a valley from a bay on the northern shore of the island. Its massive stone temple protruded awkwardly from the cliff face at the upper end of the valley and served as the central meeting place for formal ceremonies and official assemblies. Half of the structure was buried deep in the cliff, providing secluded shelter for Bishain, the high-elder, and his family. The other half of the temple projected from the cliff face like a huge stone snout looming over the village. In Tangar's mind, it served as an awkward reminder of the forgotten artistry of their ancestors to be able to carve a single stone into such a perfectly formed edifice.

The central courtyard opened unto the sky with three terraced mounds dedicated to growing special herbs and spices. After the autumn harvest, the stone utility platforms atop each mound were adorned with carpets and flowers, transforming them into symbolic vessels containing the souls in the bonding ceremony.

The village itself clustered around the temple with markets and shops, while farms and houses sprawled down the fertile slope to the sea. As the outlying tribes gathered each year, the farmland became an untidy jumble of makeshift tents and athletic fields where competitive games took place.

This year, the games culminated with Stafon winning third-runner-up in the spear throw and he managed to convince Laura to bond with him. Talbot still found women too baffling and Tangar celebrated his fourth year with Tarann so it was generally a good time had by all.

After much deliberation, Nolan determined that his three novitiates were able, if not eager, to accept the teachings of 'the way' laid out in the sacred scrolls. He favored Talbot's frequent interactions, challenging every precept in an extended exchange of ideas while Tangar and Stafon participated somewhat passively in the indoctrination.

The classes were often held in the private quarters of the high-elder to avoid the involvement of "the few", as he called them. The sessions were mostly the repeated readings of the scrolls with countless interruptions to address Talbot's questions.

Tangar found the finer points of the text muddled in confused imagery of future times and feats of valor from some distant past. The sessions were entertaining in spite of, or perhaps because of, the secretive air of avoiding the few.

As spring approached, the gathering broke up and the trio assembled their families for the trek home. Talbot had only to turn around since he lived in the gathering village and, while Stafon had the longest route back to the western seacoast; Tangar had the more arduous journey to the high country lake.

Tarann tried to make conversation as Tangar lugged their overloaded cart along a dry creek bed. "I don't think Talbot likes me."

"Why do you say that? He just doesn't know how to talk with women."

"I don't know. Maybe he doesn't like women."

"I think he likes them too much. They scare him. He's afraid he'll say something that'll cross him up, so he just doesn't say anything. He has a lot on his mind lately."

"Like what – you three sneaking off every chance you get? I'm beginning to wonder about you guys."

"Hmm... Yes. We sort of had things to do. Training, you know."

"Training, what sort of training? Or is that a secret too?"

Tangar parked their cart, pulled the harness from his sweaty shoulders, and looked back down the trail for his father. "No, not from you... I didn't want to tell you while we were still there. We're not supposed to let anyone of the new order know that we're chosen to hold the knowledge of the old-ways. Bishain tasked Nolan to train us on the sacred scrolls. We're supposed to keep it secret until 'the one foretold' is known. I'm not sure what that means, but it's a burden trying to not say anything in front of the others. I feel like we're doing something wrong, or something."

Tarann pulled a bag of water from the cart and offered it to him. Tugging the weave of deep red hair from her shoulder, she twisted it into a tight knot on the back of her head and pinned it in place. "Well if that's all it is, I feel better. I thought you were going to put me aside in favor of someone – new. I'm sorry I haven't been able to give you the son you deserve."

He drank his fill of water, letting a good amount flow down his naked chest. "Don't be silly. You've given me more than I deserve. We'll have children when the time is right. Vau will smile upon us with a special child to grace the world in 'the way'."

"Don't talk like that. I want a baby, plain and simple. Not some mystical child troubled with keeping the stories in some old scrolls straight."

"Careful now, YodHeaVau will hear your curse and 'bless' you with children of strife."

"I'll show you strife..." She pulled the water bag from his grasp and squirted him in the face.

They tussled over the control of the water for a few moments and ended in a long embrace that was cut short by Chilbain and Catherin shuffling up the ravine with their cart.

Catherin snickered and admonished them. "Careful now, you'll end up with a gathering-child. People will talk of your indiscretion."

Tarann laughed and patted Catherin's obviously pregnant tummy. "Speaking of which, when is this little indiscretion going to show up?"

She tugged at the colorful wrap supporting her waist. "Not soon enough. I'll be no help in the first planting." The two women laughed as they sought shade under a nearby tree.

The path was wide enough for Chilbain to maneuver his cart around Tangar's, but he also opted to take a break from his toil. Shedding his harness, he turned to address Tangar. "Do you think we can get past the bush monkeys before nightfall?"

"I hope so. They don't make good bedfellows. Did you pass Pop? How far back is he?"

"Not too far. He's picking mushrooms back at that fallen tree." He gestured back down the trail.

Tangar search his cart and pulled a couple of pieces of dried meat from the bundles. He handed one to his childhood friend and tugged hard to pull a bite free. "What did you think of the enlightened ceremony this year?"

Chilbain tugged at his bit of meat. After several moments of deliberate chewing, he paused and looked skeptically at Tangar. "Not much... I mean, I guess it got the job done, but it just doesn't seem to have the – formality of the past. Don't get me wrong... There's plenty of ritual stuff, but it just doesn't – speak to me. You know what I mean?"

"Careful now, you're talking heresy to doubt the enlightened way."

"Enlightened my ass. I haven't noticed any enlightenment in my life."

"It's not your life they're enlightening. Never mind. I'm just bitter with all the new rules."

"Yeah, I know what you mean. I mean, I don't mind giving a gift of respect to the elders, but those crooks picked through our stuff and took Catherin's favorite blanket. It was her mother's. They don't have the right to just take whatever they want."

"Well, actually, under the enlightened way, they do. They said, 'it's for the betterment of us all that they take things of pride and give them to the deserving among us'."

"Betterment huh? What's better about giving my wife's treasure to a temple maiden? I saw one of those girls wearing it like a badge of honor. What did she do to deserve such a gift?"

"I'm sure she did something very nice for the elders but it's best not to dwell on such things. Have you settled things with Lambert? I noticed him giving you a hard time about something."

"He's another one... He thinks he can just lie around drinking and I'm supposed to kiss his ass just because he's a master hunter. So, he's a better shot than I am. That doesn't mean I have to let him push me around. He stepped on my foot at the bonding ceremony and didn't even say boo, go to hell, or anything."

"Maybe he didn't know he did it."

"He probably didn't. He was drunk, but that doesn't make it OK. That makes it worse to my way of thinking."

Tarann approached, offering the bladder of water. "Are you rested?"

Chilbain nodded toward Catherin. "Yeah, it's about that time. Come on old girl. We need to get past those monkeys."

Tangar smiled at his wife's timid dominance. "Yeah, we'll be along as soon as Dad catches up and I talk him into riding for a while."

Tarann stuffed the last pieces of winter clothes into her cedar chest and sat gazing wistfully at the remaining bundle. It was folded neatly and tied with a bit of ribbon. She caressed the cloth as a tear formed. The yet unused baby clothes were a gift from her mother, just before she died, and are her most prized possession. They aren't anything special. They're made for the rugged utility that her mother knew an active baby would need, but to her they are the most precious things she has ever known. She placed them reverentially on the top of the other clothes and closed the lid of the chest. She knew they would be safe there and perhaps, next winter when she opened the chest, they would be needed.

She whispered the prayer she had said so many times before. "Please dear Vau, mother of all life, I beg You to fulfill my wish. Please, please..."

She couldn't think of anything else to say as tears began to warmly caress her checks. *Maybe Tangar's right. Maybe all my prying will bring a special child. I fear what that could mean. I just want a normal baby to grow with, not some wizard of forbidden knowledge.*

Tangar had finished the final setting of tent stays and entered their newly erected hut. "That should hold it for a while."

She pushed the chest aside and rubbed the tears from her face. "Sometimes I hate you."

He was taken aback but quickly assessed her feelings. "Well, as long as it's only sometimes I guess we'll be OK."

She dodged his grasp as he tried to pull her close to his sweaty frame. "Do you blame me?"

"Blame you for what? I can't think of anything I blame you for except maybe throwing out my smoking herb."

"For not giving you a son. For not being the wife you deserve."

"We've already talked about that. I don't blame you. I could never blame you for such a thing, besides, maybe it's my fault. Do you blame me for not giving you the child you want?"

"I don't know... No of course not. It's just that I want to be a mother so badly. I don't feel like I'm really your wife if I can't give you a child. Maybe you should take another woman that can be what I can't."

"I don't want another woman. We'll have children. Pop says that it's in the scrolls. We'll have a son that is 'the man foretold' and a daughter that will be 'the mother of the one who will walk proudly in the sun'."

"No! Don't curse us with such nonsense. I don't want some fulfillment of your dumb scrolls. I want normal children that'll learn to play and have faults just like any other children."

She nearly broke into tears again but pulled herself together and shoved the storage chest at him. "Put this away and fetch some water." She turned away from his gaze and dug into the remaining household goods she was unpacking. Pulling a small leather pouch from the clutter, she placed it on top of the chest.

He recognized it immediately as his smoking herb.

The newly acquired knowledge of the sacred scrolls weighed heavily on Tangar. "It isn't that they're complicated or full of great wisdom. If anything, they seem trivial to me... I mean, they're just a jumble of parables and metaphors. At least I think they are. I just want to talk with someone about them. With all the secrecy and all, I can't trust Molar. I'm afraid he's too deeply-rooted in the enlightened way. I mean, despite him being my mentor, I just don't trust him."

Tarann sat patiently listening but didn't really understand the turmoil he felt. "Maybe you can talk with Chilbain. You two get along. Maybe he can help."

"Yeah, maybe... I guess it doesn't really matter. I mean, it doesn't really have anything to do with anything. They're just a bunch of stories that don't make much sense anyway. Maybe the enlightened path is right for us now. Maybe the old-ways have passed and should be forgotten. I mean, it's not like God seems to care one way or the other. Maybe they're right. Maybe He's dead, like they say."

"Talk with your dad. He's read them hasn't he? I mean, he was a Seer. He should know all about them. He'll, at least, understand your concern."

"Yeah, I guess. In the meantime, I have to go help Molar. One of the Blain kids stepped on something. I have to show him that I know what to do."

***

Molar looked critically at the young girl, sat back from the task, and addressed Tangar. "It looks to be a tasson thorn. Show me how to handle it."

Tangar gently stroked and prodded the tender flesh of her foot. "Well, Barb, how did this happen?"

She wiped a tear from her cheek and timidly whispered. "We were just walking up along Hogback ridge and all of the sudden my foot started to hurt. I'm going to be OK aren't I? I mean, it's just a thorn isn't it?"

"Hmm. Yes, I think you're going to be OK if you tell me the truth. Was there running involved? Maybe some running off the trail with one of the Rancon boys?"

The girl whimpered tearfully as Tangar used the delicate edge of an obsidian blade to open the wound. Quickly grabbing a salve he had prepared, he spread it into the wound. The bleeding quickly stopped but her whimpers turned to earnest cries of pain. "Stop! Stop it... It stings. It really hurts."

As the salve numbed her foot, he prodded the wound with a pair of exquisitely thin bone fragments. Skillfully trapping the end of the thorn between the probes, he slowly extracted it and held it up to the light. He carefully assessed the condition of the spine. "I think we got most of it."

He cleaned the wound vigorously, applied some additional salve, and wrapped it tightly to hold the wound closed. "Now if you promise to not go running off trail again, I'll let you go."

Barb did her best to seem brave. "I promise."

Scooping some salve into a cup he handed it to her mother. "Keep her off her feet for three days. Clean the wound with boiled water and apply this cream twice a day. Wrap her foot tightly to hold the wound closed and if it swells or she gets a fever come back right away."

As the family awkwardly limped out of the Seer's hut Molar picked up the thorn and felt the end of the barb. "It's not very sharp. You probably missed the tip."

"I know. It'll fester out in a few days."

"Or, she'll get infected and I'll have to operate. You should have dug it out."

"I think she'll be alright. She's young. If it starts to swell, I'll open it up again and let it drain."

Molar scoffed at his optimism as he drew hard on a cup of tea. "You think... You think... You ignore my years of experience and pretend to know how a young girl has strayed. Well, you handle it then. And when she dies of fever, you can tell her parents that **you thought** she'd be OK."

Tangar ignored his customary critical comment and tried to change the subject. "You're on the high council, have you ever studied the old-ways?"

"God no! Why should I? It's just a bunch of superstitious nonsense. The council put it aside years ago. Why do you ask?"

"Oh, nothing. It just came up at the gathering. Some of the other guys asked about it. That's all."

"Well, you best leave that old crap alone if you know what's good for you. No benefit can come of it. You tell your friends to stay clear of that stuff or they'll find themselves on the outside looking in. They'll go from apprentice shaman to picking weeds for the women in the blink of an eye."

"Is it that bad? I mean, what could it possibly say that's so bad?"

"It says the high council doesn't know what they're talking about and that you're out of a good job."

"I gotcha, wouldn't want to upset the big guys. I was just curious that's all."

"You just study the things I've given you and don't worry about that old crap. Have you gotten that torish root I told you to go find?"

"Ah, no... I was sort of waiting for a cool day. That's a long walk for this time of year."

"Well, pull the guide stick for it and do it... When I tell you to do something, I want it done. It's not up to you to decide when." Molar grabbed his medicine pouch and tossed it to him as he stepped out the door.

Tangar grabbed the pouch out of midair and resolved to do as he was told, despite his resentment of the old man's authority. Digging through the pouch he quickly extracted the medicine cloth and started sorting through the jumble of guide sticks it contained. It surprised him how few Molar had. *Dad's collection is easily twice the size and is always neatly sorted into summer and winter bundles. Molar's set is just a bunch of crudely carved sticks tossed loosely into the cloth. It too is a poor example of artistry. The sunburst design is nothing more than a crude circle with notches fit into the edge representing the trails out of the village.*

He knew the torish wand was one of the longer sticks so he quickly found it and placed it on the cloth being sure it fit into the notch for the eastern trail. Grumbling at the prospect, he rolled up the cloth. "It measures out to be over two weeks in each direction to find this stuff. What's the big rush to get torish-root? If I remember right, he uses it to brew the spirit-tea him and his buddies drink after everyone else has gone to bed. Great, I get to spend a month traipsing around the countryside so he can get drunk with his friends. I guess it's penance for asking him questions he can't answer."

Chilbain pulled his shoe on. "You want to what?"

"It's more of 'need' than want. I have to go get some herb for Molar. He sort of made a big deal about it, so I have to step and fetch it or he's going to find someone else who will."

"Still, that's a damn long walk for some old weed. Can't you just slip him some mushrooms and be done with it?"

"Come on. You know I can't. I need someone to cover my back."

"Yeah, alright. Catherin will be bent that I'm not here to listen to her complaining about the baby but a nice walkabout will keep me out of her way for a while."

"Ah, good, I knew you could help. We'll get an elk or something on the way home. That should make her happy."

"Nothing will make her happy except having the baby. That's all she thinks about. I guess I can't blame her. It consumes her."

"Yeah, it's all Tarann thinks about too, and she's not even pregnant. Maybe that's worse. Women are funny that way."

"Funny isn't the word for it. Cat's as serious as a stab wound about it and it's really hard to get anything else done."

"Just the same, I really need someone to come with me. It's too dangerous to hunt alone. Tell her Molar has commanded me to go and wants you to come along to protect me."

"Hmm... She doesn't think much of Molar either. Seer or not, she thinks he's a drunken old letch that doesn't serve the community well by drinking spirit-tea all night and sleeping all day."

"Yeah, there are a lot of people that don't agree with the ways of the new order. Well, I'm sure she'll be happy to know that the herb we're going to get is for his tea."

***

Tarann looked up from her weaving. "You're what? Are you crazy? What about the Blain girl? Are you going to let Molar handle that?"

"Yeah, I don't have much choice. He got all pissy when I asked him about the old-ways and gave me this mission. I think he's testing my loyalty."

"I thought you were going to talk to your dad about it, not Molar."

"It just sort of slipped out. Besides, Dad's a little hard to talk to these days. He doesn't hear half of what I say, and doesn't seem to answer questions. He just pulls out that old talking stick of his and starts driveling on about some parable... It seems like he only has about three stories and I've heard them all too many times. You know what I mean? It's just hard to listen to his wanderings."

"I don't know. He sounds like the perfect guy to talk to about the old-ways."

"Yeah, you're probably right, but what's done is done. I have to go fetch some herb to prove to Molar that I'm worthy and can read his dumb guide stick. I should learn to keep my mouth shut."

"You said it. You know Catherin's going to be mad at you, don't you? I mean, she'll mostly be mad at Chilbain, but there'll be plenty to go around for you."

"Yeah – I don't suppose you'd talk to her for me. I mean, I need someone to come with me through lion country and Chilbain's my best bet."

"Oh no! I don't want to get on her bad side. She's baby-crazy. She'll rip me apart because I'm not a mother and I 'can't possibly understand'. I don't want to face that kind of abuse."

"I know. I'm sorry. I didn't mean to bring all that up, but she isn't due yet. Why is she all worked up?"

"It's different for everyone. She feels the stress more than most. She'll get better as her time approaches."

"Maybe it'll be good for her to be on her own. Maybe she'll find solace with some time to herself."

"Yeah, and maybe pigs will fly. No. I'm afraid you're going to have to convince her that you need Chilbain more than she does."

"No problem. She'll be mad enough at him, she'll be glad to see him go."

***

Tangar stood submissively just inside the door of Chilbain's hut. "... So you see, I need a trusted companion on this urgent mission and Chilbain is the best marksman I know. I'm sure Molar will be grateful for your sacrifice and will compensate you generously."

Catherin sat awkwardly on a pillow near her hearth. "Yeah, like what? I don't need a bunch of worthless chants from that old sot. And, what if my baby comes while you're gone? Who will tend my needs?"

Chilbain knelt next to her. "I'll be back before the baby comes. We'll make it quick and I'll bring you an elk hide from the lowlands. You'll thank me this winter."

"I'll thank you to not go. Let this fool run his own errands."

"It's too dangerous; I've already said I'll help. You don't want me to go back on my word do you?"

"You give your word too freely to this charlatan. The planting isn't done yet and he wants to go traipsing off in search of some weed so he and his master can sit around dreaming of ghosts and spirits."

Tangar winced at the assault. "I assure you the herb we are sent to retrieve is of great importance to the wellbeing of us all. It is a sacrament that must be made before the final planting to assure a good harvest and healthy children. You don't want to stand in the way of bringing healthy children into the world."

"What a line of crap. You know as well as I do that Molar just wants some weed he can smoke, or drink, or something, so he can escape work in the name of Yod. Well, go! I'm tired of arguing with you. See if I care when you miss the birth of your son. We'll get along fine without you. I'll find someone else that'll be happy to care for me and my baby."

***

Tangar dropped his pack near a large rock that served as a windbreak. "This will do for the night, unless you have a better idea."

"Hmm." Chilbain searched the site and decided that while it wasn't very flat, it did offer some shelter from the incessant wind coming down the valley.

Tangar set to work getting a fire started. "You're not very talkative today."

"Not much to say I guess. I keep thinking about Cat and the baby. I think maybe I shouldn't have come."

"Yeah, that didn't go as well as I'd hoped, but she'll be OK. She's a good woman. I asked Tarann to talk with her. That should help."

Chilbain scoffed at his optimism. "Easy for you to say... I'm the one that's going to have to live with her."

"She'll forget all about it as soon as the baby comes. You'll both be too busy to be mad."

"Speaking of which, what's your problem? You need a little less training on potions and a little more training in the bed?"

"I guess... Tarann blames herself for not being able to have kids. I don't know if it's her or me. We keep trying, but it just doesn't seem to happen."

"Too many nights with Molar... All those potions and teas can't be good for you."

"Maybe you're right. It sure hasn't done him any good. He's getting to the point that he doesn't make sense some of the time. That's not a good thing when he's trying to teach me some potion or something."

"How can you tell? He's never made much sense to me."

"It's like he's trying to make things harder than they need to be. Maybe he's just testing me to see if I'm listening. He'll tell me one thing, and then he'll do something different when he demonstrates. Like he's trying to trick me."

"Maybe it doesn't make any difference. I mean, maybe three or four pinches of stump-weed doesn't make any difference to your witches brew."

"Very funny... I'll remember that the next time you come to me with a stomachache."

"You know what I mean. Maybe you can adjust the amounts a little based on the need."

"Yeah, sure, but this is different. He doesn't seem to even recognize that he's done it. He just carries on as if nothing's wrong."

"Do you call him on it? Maybe that's what he wants."

"Yeah, but that's a fine line. That's how I got stuck with this stupid assignment. If I ask him something he can't answer, he gets all pissy and threatens to dump me. It's like he's looking to find fault."

"Why don't you just give it up? Let someone else do all that mumbo-jumbo. You're a good enough shot to make a living on one of the hunting teams."

"I'm my father's son. He's the real Seer, not Molar. I learned more from him in a day than I've learned from Molar in two years. His spirit calls to me to takeover for him, as I should. I just wish all this political crap of the enlightenment would go away. I mean, I don't care about all that. If their way works better than the old-ways, great... It just doesn't seem to. I mean, I know the old-ways had a lot of chanting and praying that didn't seem to do anything, but the enlightened ways seem to just be a bunch of shaman drinking spirit-tea and telling each other how clever they are. That's not much use to the sick."

"Careful now... Talk like that will get you more of these assignments of futile valor."

Chilbain prodded the fire and edged an ember into the carrying pot. "How much further?"

Tangar gazed thoughtfully up the trail, packed his bedroll away, and pulled the guide stick from his pack. Lamenting the quality of workmanship, he grumbled. "Looks to be another day or two, if I'm reading this correctly."

"What do you mean 'if'?"

"Well you know how it is... This little knob could be that hill over there, or it could be that one over there." He pointed the stick to a nearby hill and then to one on the far horizon.

Chilbain scoffed at his apparent confusion and lit his pipe. "I thought you knew where you're going."

"Take it easy. We'll get there. What's the matter, don't you trust me?"

"Trust has nothing to do with it. I just want to get this over with. I need to get back before the baby comes."

Tangar relieved himself on the embers. "Yeah, I'll be glad to be done with this too. I've about had it with Molar's games. He loads me up with trivial crap like this, then ridicules me for not keeping up."

"Yeah, I've heard all that. What are you going to do about it? Bellyaching to me doesn't get you anywhere; man-up and stop complaining."

Tangar clinched the guide stick in his fist and considered the words of his friend. "You're right, but that doesn't mean I want to hear about it. I mean, what am I supposed to do? If I tell Molar to hang it up, he'll either dump me or make things worse."

"You're still just complaining. I can't help you. Don't get me wrong, I would if I could, but all that Seer crap is beyond me. It's all a bunch of mumbo-jumbo. Talk to your dad, he used to be one, or maybe one of the other shaman would know what to do."

"There are only two others that would understand and they're both too far away."

"Well, there you are then. You want to be a shaman. You're supposed to be able to talk with the gods. Ask Yod what to do."

"I have. He just told me to man-up."

"Sounds like a plan. Come on. Let's get moving." Chilbain blew smoke through his pipe, emptying it, and slipped it into his herb pouch. Scattering the last vestiges of the morning fire with the butt of his spear, he headed up the trail.

Tangar took one last look at the guide stick and stuffed it into his pack. "So, what are you going to do about Lambert? You two don't seem to get along very well."

"What's to do? He's a drunken lout. I stay as far away from him as I can and as long as he doesn't push his privileged attitude on me, I guess I don't care."

"He seems to have friends in high places. I mean, he can make it tough on you come harvest time."

"Just because his father was on the council doesn't give him the right to tell me what to do."

"No. It doesn't give him the right, but it gives him influence on the harvest committee. If they give you that rocky patch up on the hill, you're going to go hungry come winter."

"If he does, so be it. I'll have a heart-to-heart talk with him on our next hunt together."

"I don't think I want to hear about it. In the meantime, I have to figure out what to do about the old-ways."

"What's to figure? The high council has 'awoken unto the light'. Isn't that what they say? They have spoken with the gods and lowly people like us don't need to concern ourselves with such things. They'll do the right thing for the betterment of us all."

"Yeah, it's funny how they claim to have spoken to the gods in one breath and then they claim there is no god in the next breath. They have a very convenient god."

The next few hours passed in silence as the two men made their way through lion country. On several occasions, they stopped to gauge movements and noises in the undergrowth but no cat presented itself.

Shortly after the midday break, they came upon a fork in the trail. Tangar pulled the guide stick out and puzzled over the knobs and notches crudely etched into the sprig. "I think we're here." He rubbed his finger along the shaft. "We should take the left trail here and keep an eye out for a fork back to the right in about an hour."

Chilbain looked solemnly up the narrow overgrown path, handed his spear to Tangar, and pulled his bow from around his chest. Fitting an arrow to the string, he gave a 'be quiet' gesture and motioned for him to stay back. Cautiously moving along the arroyo, he listened intently for movement in the brush.

Tangar recognized his superior hunting skills and tucked a spear under each arm in a rather comical defensive posture. Lagging back to stay clear of Chilbain's wary movements, he cautiously followed him up the trail keeping an eye out for a rear assault.

The new growth of tall grass encroaching from the left drew Chilbain's attention. The movement was irregular rather than windblown waves. He slowly exhaled, drawing his bow to full extension. After several moments of frozen assessment, he relaxed his stance and lowered his aim. Hollering at the top of his lungs, he quickly picked up a stone and tossed it into the weeds. A young cat dashed across the path and disappeared down the arroyo in a blur of lean tan fur. "Keep an eye out. Its mother is probably around here somewhere."

As the ravine opened into what could only be called a gorge, Chelbain eased his vigil. The likelihood of a cat surprising them lessened as the canyon walls spread up and away. "I think we'll be OK now, but you can carry my spear, just the same."

"Hmm, and you can..." Tangar grumbled under his breath as he juggled the spears while attempting to take a swig of water. "I think that arroyo up there might be the turn we need to make. It's going in the right direction, and looks like it might lead us out of this ditch."

"Yeah, good. So what's this weed we're looking for look like?"

Tangar fumbled with the spears and pulled the guide stick from his pack. Fingering the blunt end of the wand for a moment, he looked dismayed. "Hmm – not very helpful. I don't know where Molar got this stick but it's not carved very well. It looks like it has five leaves or maybe five points on each leaf. I'll know when I see the root."

"You don't even know what we're looking for?"

"I've seen the root before. Molar has it all stripped down to nothing but the root by the time he uses it. That's what I'm supposed to be learning I guess. 'The journey sweetens the fruit of knowledge.' They always say."

"What a load of crap. A fifty-mile hike and now you tell me you don't even know what you're looking for. You and your mysteries of the shaman... Just let me know when you've dug up the right weed."

The struggle up the steep sandy embankment of the arroyo left both men sweaty and covered in a light dusting of fine white pumice. The grassy plain that spread out before them was spotted with clumps of trees and bushes that promised hours of tedious horticulture trying to find the vaunted torish-root.

Tangar tried to hide his dismay. "Well, we made it. It should only take a couple of minutes to find the right one."

Chilbain brushed vainly at the dust on his legs. "You do that. I'll be right here getting a fire started."

By the time Tangar returned with a couple of likely plants, Chilbain had gotten a rabbit and started cooking it. "I think this is it. The light's getting bad, so it's a little hard to tell, but this looks to be right."

By way of celebration they each ate their fill and smoked a couple of pinches of herb around the fire. As the sun began to set, Tangar stripped the branches from his prize and placed them one by one on the flames while chanting... "Thank you Vau for the gift of knowledge You bring us."

"Vau? What sort of prayer is that?"

"It's of the old-ways. She is the mother of all life. The One who has smiled on this humble plant to bring Her knowledge of the Spirit, Yod."

"Old-ways? That's going to get you into trouble isn't it?"

"Not unless you tell someone and I trust you won't."

"Humph... Do you trust that this is the right weed?"

"Yeah, I've been thinking about that. I have to be sure it's the right one so I guess I'm going to have to test it... It's part of the job."

"What do you mean 'test it'? If you think I'm going to eat any of that you're crazy."

"No. It's a spirit herb. Only the shaman is worthy of its knowledge."

"Sounds like a load of crap to me. Does that mean you're going to eat it?"

"Well, drink it actually. 'A simple tea to finish the meal and refresh the spirit'."

Taking the trunk of the plant, he cut the root off and placed the stalk reverentially on the fire. Over the next few minutes, he chanted a rhythmic tune while slicing, dicing, and mashing the root into a paste that he then brewed in hot water and strained into a cup.

Chilbain watched the procedure with amusement that his old friend had learned such a colorful process. "You're going to make Tarann a good wife someday."

"Yeah, it's a fine skill honed while slaving over the kitchen fire." He twisted the filter cloth to squeeze the last drop from the mash. "Now, if this doesn't kill me, I'll have my answer."

"If it kills you, I'm leaving you here. I don't want to be seen with a fool that poisons himself."

Tangar smiled slightly at his friend's apprehension. "I don't blame you. I wouldn't want to be seen with a fool like me either."

He sniffed at the cup before him. The smell reminded him of rancid pumpkin. He closed his eyes and took the smallest sip he could manage of the hot liquid. The taste of pumpkin he was expecting lost out immediately to raw potatoes. It wasn't as bad as he had anticipated, but it wasn't going to be high on his favored menu. The sip spread to the back of his tongue and down his throat. He nearly retched as the spoiled pumpkin returned to his nose.

"Well, are you going to die?"

"I don't think so. I may puke, but I don't think it'll kill me." He sipped again on the edge of the cup making a slurping sound. "Hmm, yes, that's really bad. Maybe if I just gulp it down."

"Yeah, and maybe I'll have to spend the next three days watching you barf your guts up."

"A small price to pay for the knowledge of the gods."

"Is that the line of crap they feed you to rationalize poisoning yourself?"

"It's the line of crap they use to disguise their fondness of the condition. Don't get me wrong... There's a place for each of the 'poisons', as you call them, but I'm afraid many of the enlightened-way have found the herbs too – attractive, too comfortable. They use them to escape the burdens of the Seer."

Tangar continued to sip cautiously at the brew. "I've seen many good men grow dependent on the comfort of forgetfulness. They –, we, are asked to make many difficult decisions and sometimes there are regrettable consequences. It changes a man. The strong become weak, the determined hesitate, the good find reasons to listen to bad counsel. The really bad thing is that they don't recognize that they've changed."

"Then why do you do it? Why not just let Molar and his kind play at their game? It doesn't matter to people like me. I do my job and they leave me alone. Life goes on."

"Good questions. See, already the potion loosens my tongue. I'll tell you something that you can't reveal to anyone – I've been chosen to carry the knowledge of the old-ways."

"Yeah, so? Old-ways, new-ways, it's all the same. I don't care how enlightened they say they are. Some guy sets himself up in charge and everyone else has to bow down and kiss his – ring. There's nothing new about that."

"No. That's just it. It's not about being in charge. It's, it's..." Tangar's eyes drifted off into the distance. After several minutes of silence, he looked back at the fire. "What was I saying?"

"Beats the hell out of me. I think you were going to tell me that the tea wasn't doing anything to you."

"Yeah, probably." He took another sip of the now lukewarm potion. "The way I look at it, if I'm supposed to learn all the stuff in those scrolls, I'm going to have to..." Again, his eyes drifted off into the distance and he fell silent.

Chilbain took the cup from his hand, sniffed at the gray liquid, and emptied it into the nearby bush. "I think we can safely say that you found the right weed."

Chilbain stirred the fire to life and began to prepare the snake he had caught just before dawn. "You look like crap. Any great words of wisdom you want to impart from your spirit walk?"

Tangar rose solemnly and sat bleary eyed in the column of smoke. "I feel worse than I look and, no, the only wisdom I gained is to not drink that stuff."

"You're never going to fit in with the other shaman with an attitude like that."

Tangar moved to avoid the smoke and bent to prepare his morning tea. The smoke followed him and somehow seemed worse than before. "Fitting in with that bunch of layabouts is the least of my problems. I'm pretty sure that was the herb I was sent for, but I'm not sure what I'm supposed to have learned from it. I mean, sure I followed his crappy guide stick, found the plant, and prepared the potion, but so what? It just doesn't seem worthwhile to come all this way just to brew bad tea."

"Maybe that's the lesson. You did your master's bidding. Now show your commitment to the enlightenment by returning with an ample supply of stinkweed to cement your position in their club."

Tangar moved again to avoid the smoke and sipped at his tea in silence. After several moments, he squinted through the smoke that had again followed him. "I don't want to join their club. I want to do as my father did. He led his people through wisdom and sacrifice. The herbs were just a necessary sacrament that he performed as a solemn duty, not selfish amusement."

"Don't tell me. I just watched you do something very foolish. I can't pretend to understand your reasoning in doing it. Maybe it was as noble as your father's sacrifice or maybe it was just curious self-indulgence. It doesn't matter to me. It's you that must know. I can only tell you that it's very dangerous. I had to stand watch all night alone while you talked to the stars. Look what it's done to your father. He talks only with the aid of his story wand, and makes no sense to any but the children. Is that the life you wish for yourself?"

Tangar picked up a stick and prodded the fire releasing a shower of sparks. "Of course not… I'll not take these herbs lightly. I know the danger of their seduction. I've seen it firsthand. I know what I'm doing."

"And he didn't?"

"He, he... He fell to the council's pressure. The enlightened pressed him to do things he knew were unwise by shaming him. They claimed it was his duty to follow their new ways. He's too old to stand up to them."

"Too old, too weak, too prideful... How is that different from what you've just done?"

"I did what I needed to do. I need to learn of these herbs so that I can use them wisely. It's part of the job. I'm not like you. I can't just put my foot down and tell them to go away. I need to know these things so that I can take my father's place. Molar shouldn't be the Seer of the lakeshore tribe. He's an outsider. He isn't one of us. He doesn't care for the people as he should. The high council picked him. They pushed my father out before his time so that they could be sure their path of enlightenment is followed. That's what ruined him. He was a good man until they shamed him."

"I know you don't respect Molar and yet you do his bidding. Am I to respect that? Am I to want you as Seer of our clan even though you don't stand up to this outsider?"

Tangar slammed his fire prod down into the embers sending a great cloud of sparks and ash into the air. "You don't understand. The time isn't right. I need to learn more, and the high council must recognize me."

"You're right. I don't understand. The high council must be made to recognize you. They'll not do it on their own. They are nothing but cowards hiding behind their ceremonies and robes: leaders of sheep. Are you a sheep, or will you stand up for our people?"

Tangar stood and relieved himself on the meager fire. It hissed and steamed as he turned to pack his remaining things. "Let's get going. I'm done with this task."

"Not so fast. Aren't you forgetting something? These weeds aren't going to dig themselves up."

Molar inspected the torish-roots. "You only brought three. I'll have to send you back when this runs out."

Tangar resented his casual dominance. "What's the correct number for your – habit?"

"You should temper your tongue. My 'habit' is to use the correct herb befitting the need. If I say I need more, then, I need more. You're not to question it. Your questioning of my wisdom has led to the Blain girl losing her foot."

"What! She was fine. What happened?"

"I told you, you should have dug that thorn out. But, you questioned it. By the third day, her foot swelled and I had to fix your shoddy work."

"What do you mean it swelled? Of course, it swelled. That doesn't mean you should cut it off for God's sake. It's supposed to swell. That means it's healing. What's wrong with you?"

"I've seen infection many more times than you, and she needed to have her foot removed. That was the only way to save her."

Tangar ran across the village commons and approached the girls hut. Slowing to a stop, he tapped gently on the doorframe. "Excuse me, can I speak with Barb? I want to see how she's doing."

Her mother looked up from her weaving. "You! You've nearly killed her. Get out of my sight!"

"Mrs. Blain, I'm so sorry, but it's not my fault. I..."

"I don't want to hear it! Get out. Leave us alone." She threw the basket she had been working on at him.

He didn't even attempt to block the assault, hoping it would somehow soothe her pain. "Please, let me see what that old fool has done. Maybe I can help."

"Molar has already done all that can be done after you botched the job. He told us how you failed to remove the thorn correctly and how it poisoned her. She's lucky he was able to save her."

Tangar grimaced in frustration and left. Molar was talking with Lambert near the central hearth. They watched his progress across the commons and exchanged snickers at his impotence.

Standing in Chilbain's hut, he was near hysterics trying to explain his torment. "... I might be able to help her. But her mom won't let me near her. Molar has poisoned her mind. He said I messed up, but I didn't! I know I didn't. She'd be better by now if he'd left her alone. Her life is ruined. Someone should cut his foot off."

Chilbain tugged thoughtfully on his pipe. "Sounds like a plan. You want to do it or shall I?"

Tangar fought back a smirk. "Yeah, it would serve him right, but right now he's hanging out with Lambert. I think he figures he'll protect him from me."

"Yeah, he showed up this morning and said I need to put a team together to go to the elk meadow. I have a pregnant wife to tend to. I can't go running off with a bunch of his loser buddies."

"What did he say to that?"

"He said... It doesn't matter what he said. I'm not going. He may be a master hunter, but that doesn't mean I have to listen to his line of crap."

"I suppose not, as long as you don't mind getting on his shit list."

"I'm already on it. So what can be done for the Blain girl?"

"I don't know. Maybe nothing but I'd, at least, like to look at it. I mean, Molar has never been good at that sort of thing. I hope he hasn't done too much damage."

"What's 'too much'? Missing a foot is pretty bad. I mean, she'll not be able to work the fields as she should. What's to become of her?"

"I don't know. With time, maybe she'll adapt. The real problem will be the gathering journey. She'll need to be carried. I'm not sure her folks are up to that. They already have two young ones to handle."

Chilbain tapped the residue from his pipe. "We'll figure out something. Maybe she'll be able to use a crutch well enough by then."

"In the meantime, that fool Molar wants me to go back and get more torish-root. I think he just wants to get me out of the way while he covers his tracks."

"Well count me out. Cat would kill me for even thinking about it."

"Yeah, how's she doing? She should be just about ready by now shouldn't she?"

"She's been 'ready' for months. I'm the one that's not ready."

"So, what're you going to do about Lambert?"

"Same thing you're going to do about Molar – nothing. I guess I'll have to do something, but I'm not sure what. Maybe I should get some of that muskroot you picked. That'd slow him down some."

"Hmm – but he's not worthy of the awakening. According to the enlightened council, 'only the truly worthy shall awaken unto the light of the new way'."

"And what's that got to do with drinking a bunch of skunkweed?"

"It **is** the new way. 'Drink of the nectar of truth and you shall awaken unto the light'."

"What a bunch of crap. It just gives them an excuse to sit around drinking that crap and passing judgment on those they decide are unworthy."

"Yeah, their hypocrisy is surpassed only by their greed."

"They revel in their hypocrisy. It flaunts their power over us. They know they're wrong but that's the point. They get away with it and you can't do anything about it. It's **that** power they covet."

Yeah, it's a bitch being on the outside. I don't suppose you want to come with me up by the falls?"

"I don't dare. Cat would have both of our heads if I traipse off with you again. We'd both be on her list."

"I'm afraid I've been on her list for quite some time. She doesn't appreciate the things I have to do to learn the ways of a Seer."

"What's to learn? You grew up with one. You should have all that mumbo-jumbo down by now."

"Yeah, it's different now. The 'old-ways' I learned from my dad are forbidden by the enlightened-few. Now I have to learn the new ways to please them and they keep changing what that means. I mean, they tell me one thing at the gathering council and then Molar changes it when we get back here. It's like some kind of guessing game. No matter what I do, it's wrong."

Lambert drew lightly on his pipe and considered Molar's proposition. The position as his master-at-arms was a very tempting offer. He would have responsibility over sanctioned disciplinary matters and access to any surplus votive offerings. The guardian aspects of the job didn't concern him since there was little call for action, but the concept of free gifts intrigued him. He knew the offerings frequently included smoking herbs and wine that fit his appetites better than having to work for them. "And what sorts of discipline are we talking about?"

"Oh, nothing major. It's really more of a show than expecting any real conflict. The high council decided that each enlightened Seer should have their tribe's best huntsman at his side to present a – 'dignified' face to the people. You know, sort of, an honorary guardian to show everyone that the council is behind him and approves of all that he does."

"And when does this show begin?"

"As soon as you pledge your allegiance to the high council and vow to uphold the teachings of the enlightened way."

"Yeah, sure. What does that mean, 'allegiance' and what 'teachings'? I'm not much on studying a bunch of scrolls."

"Allegiance simply means you'll do as I say and not question it, and I'll explain the teachings as they come up. You don't need to worry about that."

"So, just stand there and shut up... I think I can handle that. When do I get paid for this unquestioning loyalty?"

Molar leaned back and pulled a wine skin from behind a stack of firewood. "Then I have your word?"

He scoffed. "My word? Of course, you have my word that I'll do whatever you pay me for."

Molar looked skeptically at his new colleague and handed the wine to him. "Let's just start with a simple show of support. Stand with me tonight at the watch-standers' briefing. Don't drink that until we're done."

Lambert looked disappointed at the wine skin and replaced the stopper he had already removed. "Whatever you say... I'll see you later."

***

The watch-standers' briefing was about to begin when Lambert showed up at Molar's door. He was dressed in his hunting garb and carried his spear, as would be expected of a watch-stander, but had obviously opened the wine.

Molar wore the garish robes of the Seer and looked disdainfully at his new cohort. "I told you not to drink that wine until this is over."

"I didn't drink **that** wine. I drank my own wine." He planted the butt of his spear arrogantly at his feet.

"Here wear this." Molar handed a leather sash to him.

The garment pulled easily over his head and stretched across his chest in a wide band of unblemished dignity. "Nice touch, if a bit plain."

"It fits the purpose. Now sober up and act like the man you pretend to be."

Lambert pulled his spear to bear and brought the sculpted stone tip threateningly close to Molar's throat. "The man I am has no need for your taunts. You should remember that."

"And so you'll learn the first lesson of the enlightened way... I am the Seer of this tribe, ordained by the high council to awaken a few select men to 'The Way'. If you don't wish to be a part of the chosen few, so be it. You don't need to follow my lead, but I warn you that you'll get no comfort when you fall ill. And, I can guarantee that you **will** fall ill."

"You threaten me while I hold a blade to your throat?"

"I have no fear of your blundering ways. You can kill me, but it won't change the ways of enlightenment. You will regret your decision as your kin pay the price for your arrogance."

Lambert eased his stance and put his spear aside. "My family is of no concern to you."

"That's true. I have no regard for them whatsoever. They are your concern alone. I couldn't care less if they live or die. But if something ill should befall me, the enlightened-few will see to their wellbeing and I can assure you that you will outlive them all. For you see, the greatest strength of the enlightenment is that our followers will do what needs done without – encouragement. This gives you an incentive to keep me well for I can assure you that it's best for all concerned that you grow to embrace the warmth of this shared strength. Now, stand behind me and see to it that no one raises his hand in anger."

The men of the tribe gathered congenially around the night watchman's hearth. There were no issues to be addressed and the watchstanders had already been assigned when Molar and Lambert arrived.

The assembly grew silent at the extraordinary appearance of the pair. To have the Seer attend the routine meeting was unusual, but to have him show up in his full ceremonial dress with a master hunter acting as a guardian was unheard of.

Molar spoke clearly. "I've come to speak with you... You men are the future of our people. It's important that you, above all, understand how important it is to awaken unto the light. By that, I mean you must know the enlightened ways of our future. In the past, ignorant old men that were stuck in the old ways led our people astray. They didn't know the truth. These men read our sacred scrolls incorrectly. They thought the scrolls spoke of our future, but we now know they speak only of some long forgotten past. You must bring our future and not rely on the false readings of some ancient rags. Now we read only the scrolls of birth and death. For we now know that these are the things that concern us. These are the things of Yod's enlightened way, not the fanciful wanderings of misguided old fools."

Tangar remained at the back of the group, as was his habit. Chilbain sidled up next to him and, nudging his shoulder, whispered. "You gonna let him get away with that?"

Tangar whispered. "His ignorance is surpassed only by his arrogance."

Molar turned to face the pair. "Tangar, do you have something to add?"

Lambert pulled his spear to the ready but Molar halted his advance with a dismissive motion. The group took note of the gesture and remained silent in expectation that something more would develop.

After a moment's hesitation, Tangar spoke softly. "No. The enlightened way speaks for itself. I can add nothing to its – wisdom."

"Then remain silent! Others wish to hear of the awakening."

Chilbain casually adjusted his stance to more actively grasp his spear. "You speak of knowing the truth of the sacred scrolls yet you deny the wisdom of so many generations. You say our ancestors were wrong but, now, you're right. How can you know that? How can so many great men of our past be wrong?"

"Chilbain... You're a formidable and respected hunter, but you're not knowledgeable in the workings of the high council. We have studied this issue for many years. We have read the scrolls in great detail and walked many times with the spirit of Yod. He speaks to us now as never before, for we have awoken unto His light."

"Is this light from God or is it from too much of that stump-water you drink?"

Molar moved to put Lambert between them. "Your disrespect betrays your envy of our authority. We, of the high council, disregard such insolence as the empty bleating of ignorant sheep that are too obstinate to learn the ways of the enlightened path."

Chilbain stepped aside to get a better view of Molar. "Too obstinate to fall for a bunch of bluff and bluster. Show me in the scrolls where it says you are to lord over us, withholding what is rightfully ours. You steal my wife's blanket and give it to a temple maiden. Am I to respect that?"

Molar again moved to screen himself from assault. "You are too simple to understand the wisdom of the new way. The dues paid by someone such as you are given to the truly deserving among us. You should be honored that your contribution found favor with a simple servant girl. I'm sure she will bless your house for meeting her meager needs."

Chilbain hefted his lance and again stepped to gain access to his prey. "Stop hiding behind your temple eunuch and face me like a man."

Lambert bristled at the assault and leveled his spear unsteadily at Chilbain's chest. "You'd be wise to choose your words carefully."

"Haven't you been listening to your master? My words are of no significance to the enlightened-few. That's you isn't it? One of the chosen?" Chilbain quickly parried the spear tip with his lance and soon stood with his blade at the throat of his drunken opponent.

Tangar hefted his lance and swept the gathering of warriors before bringing it to bear on Molar. "I realize I'm only one of the ignorant sheep, but I'm an ignorant sheep that would just as soon use this blade as play word games with you."

Molar stepped to shield himself behind Lamberts befuddled hulk. "No need to get all upset. I've said what I came to say. Those of you, who are wise, will listen. Contrary to what my apprentice here says, my words are more important than you can possibly imagine. Now, heed what I've said and go about your duties."

Molar waved his scepter over the gathering as if dismissing them to do his bidding.

Tangar shuffled through his collection of trinkets looking for his pipe. The wooden bowl rattled and skidded across the packed earth floor of his hut as he pulled the ceramic cone from the jumble. "... Then Chilbain knocked his spear away and confronted him. I thought he was going to finish him off right then."

Tarann sat across the evening fire listening to his tail of adventure. "It sounds to me like you two have gotten yourselves into trouble again."

"What do you mean? We just asked a couple of questions. No one should care if we just ask a question."

"Questions he doesn't want to answer."

"Questions that need to be asked."

"You heard him. Words matter to him more than deeds. He doesn't care if you kill Lambert. He's expendable. Just don't talk about how flimsy his beliefs are."

"But don't you see? Those men need to know the things he says are worthless. They need to know the truth about Molar and his high council."

"The truth isn't his friend. You've made an enemy of him and he won't forget it."

"Oh, you worry too much. I'll just mix up some spirit-tea for him and he'll forget all about it."

Tarann gathered her things to leave. "We'll see. In the meantime, I have to go check on Catherin. She wants to have her baby."

"Yeah, that should keep Chilbain busy for a while." Tangar drew lightly on his pipe and considered what Tarann had said. *She's probably right about pissing him off. He just rubs me the wrong way. I doubt he has the guts to face me. I'll just have to watch my back.*

He replaced his pipe in his bowl of junk and noticed that his father's talking stick was amongst it. *That's a little odd. He must've forgotten it. He's been doing that a lot lately. He'll be lost if he doesn't have the damn thing the next time he starts to tell one of his stories. I wonder what he would have to say about Molar and his enlightened ways.*

He ran his thumb over the irregular bumps and notches along the length of the wand. *This belongs to the story of how his team tracked a lion into the high country, if I'm not mistaken. And, these little swirls are a cautionary tale of how the river flows when the rains have passed. They're all good stories, especially when he tells them. Action and adventure that's always followed with some truth or moral to be learned by the young.*

He marveled at how intricate and interwoven the designs were. *They **are** my father. An entire lifetime held in the palm of my hand. This is the old way. True enlightenment passed from the old, in things that mean something, not dictates contrived by the high council that benefit no one but their inner circle.*

Chilbain tapped lightly on the doorframe of the hut. "You busy?"

"Nah... Just thinking about the old man. What's up?"

"The baby's near so the women threw me out. Catherin said I should apologize to Molar and Lambert. She's afraid he'll slight us, come harvest time."

"Yeah, Tarann wasn't very happy either. They're probably right. Molar has ways of getting at you. Look what he did to Barb."

"You think he'd do that? That's pretty drastic just to make a point. I mean, he's ruined her life for nothing."

"It wasn't for nothing. I think his intent was to see her as a temple maiden, unable to do anything but cater to his perversions. She's just expendable fodder for his quest of power. He cares nothing for her. That was his way of getting at me for not bowing to him."

"Are you that important to him? I mean, when your dad got – sick and they appointed Molar to take his place, I thought it was just temporary until you pass your test or whatever it is you guys do. I mean, I always assumed you guys had that transition stuff all figured out."

"Yeah, me too, but the high council has changed all of that. Bishain has lost some influence and Stanton is pressing for the ways of the enlightenment. Their ways are very seductive to the weak minded. It makes things so easy for them. They claim absolute authority yet deny any responsibility. Everything is done in the name of the people's needs."

"What people? No one has asked me what I want."

"That's just it. The enlightened claim to know what is needed for the betterment of us all, yet the councilmen are the only ones that benefit. They say that if I come to understand their ways, I too will know how the people have benefited in so many ways they don't recognize. But, I've seen the sacred scrolls. I know what they say, and they don't say anything about enlightenment."

"So, what are you going to do about it? You going to leave Molar in your dad's place?"

Tangar looked at the stick he still held. "No. He's a shadow of what my father was. I just need to convince Bishain that I'm ready to take over. He can call Molar back and put me in charge."

"Does that mean you're going to the gathering village?"

"No. I can't. I'm needed here. I have to stay close to Molar to be sure he doesn't mess anything else up. I mean, Barb isn't out of the woods yet. His butchery is far more likely to get infected than that bit of thorn I left. I should cut his hand off so he can't do it again."

"Why don't you just brew up some of that mud he drinks and put a little extra something in it? That's what happened to your dad isn't it? Some of his concoctions got mixed up or something."

Tangar reflected on his father's condition and the myriad of herbs he had consumed as part of his duties as tribal Seer. "Yeah, that's an idea, but it would be hard to convince anyone that I know what I'm doing if I poison my teacher. No. I'm afraid it will have to be something more subtle."

"Hmm... Subtle, like cutting his hand off."

"Yeah, well I'll have to think about it. In the meantime, I need to take this back to Dad." He pointed the wand toward the door. "You want to come?"

"Nah – I need to go check on the baby."

***

Tangar made his way in the elders hut. "Hey Pop, how are you?"

Thoma sat silently alone near the far wall while two young girls tended the collection of about a dozen elders gathered around a small central hearth. He frantically searched his collection of trinkets scattered on the floor in front of him. His hair was in its usual state of disarray lending a particularly unkempt air to his disheveled appearance.

"Pop, Pop... How are you?" He stood expectantly in front of the old man.

Thoma's eyes wandered around his figure for several moments and seemed not to recognize him.

"How have you been? I brought your stick back. You must have left it the last time you visited." Tangar held the wand out to him.

Thoma squinted at his face and slowly drifted to focus on his outstretched hand. After a moment, a wide grin spread across his face and his quivering hand extended to grasp the wand. He pulled it in close to his chest and his eyes sparkled with tears. "Home."

"Yes, home... How have you been?"

He glanced cautiously at the nearby attending girl and caressed the stick warmly. Rubbing his thumb over one particular bump several times, he whispered. "Walking away."

"Hmm, yes... I'm sorry I missed you. I was busy fetching torish-root for Molar."

"Fool's tea."

"Yeah... He uses a lot of it. He claims it's a sacrament of the enlightened."

Thoma seemed to be considering his response, and then pointed meaningfully at a ridge along the length of his talking stick. "Your son bears the burden of the man foretold."

"Yeah – OK. I don't have a son, yet, unless there's something I don't know."

He continued to trace intricate bumps and notches along the length of the stick. Tapping repeatedly on one spot, he again glanced at the attending girl and spoke quietly. "The witch's burden bears the one foretold in light and grace."

"Are you talking about the sacred scrolls? I read something about a witch in one of them. It didn't make much sense to me. Say, did you know the high council has decided to scrap all but two of the scrolls. Molar said they only need the birth scroll and death scroll now. They say all of the others are outdated. I think they don't understand them, so they decided to get rid of them. Too many things they can't explain."

"Drift among clouds..."

"Yeah... People floating in the sky and living under water is just too weird. They claim the old school has read them wrong all this time and over the years has transcribed them in error. Only those who 'have awoken unto the light' can now read them properly and know they're tainted. They say they're a worthless waste of their time. They have more important things to do."

"Tea speaks."

"Yeah, I think you're right there. Speaking of bad tea, do you know of anything that can change Molar's mind without really hurting him?"

Thoma seemed to be thinking but his eyes wandered to the young girl now tending one of the elders nearby. When, at last, she finished her task he broke his gaze and once again caressed his talking wand. He pointed to a kink in the profile of the stick. "Follow the Spirit's wands. The Keeper will know His burden. Guide her warmly."

Tangar puzzled over his father's apparent loss of focus. "Yes, well, I need to be going. Please come and visit again soon. We'll talk some more. You can tell me of the Keeper's burden."

The attending girl suddenly got very busy and hurried away from where Tangar stood.

Tarann shuffled her weaving material for better access as she settled by the fire. "Chilbain's trying to figure out what he's supposed to do. It's really funny. You should go watch, besides; you need to take him a gift."

"Hmm, yeah, I guess." Tangar sorted through his medicine pouch. "Have you seen my pipe?"

"It's in there somewhere. Why don't you dump that thing and clean it? It needs it."

"Hmm, yeah, I guess. Ah, here it is." He tapped the cone on his wrist and blew through it absentmindedly as he sorted through various small packets. "Ah, yes. The tea of homage..."

***

Chilbain sat bleary eyed near the door of his hut. One of the attending women jostled him into moving out of the doorway.

Tangar approached dressed in his ceremonial robes. "Ah, I see you lived through it?"

"Yeah, more or less... It certainly was a great fuss. I'm not sure what happened, or when, but I guess I'm a father."

"How's Catherin and the baby? Have you named it yet? Is it a boy or a girl?"

"Cat's fine. It's a fine, strong, boy... Chilcoat."

"Great. Here I brought you a gift." Tangar handed him a small packet.

"Thanks. What is it?"

"It's tea. You're to drink it as part of the ceremony." Tangar whispered something to one of the attendant nurses. She smiled timidly and went into the tent.

"Tea? What kind of tea? What ceremony? What's it going to do to me?"

"Relax. It's the tea of reverence to the mother. It won't do anything to you except make you humble for what she has done for you."

The attendant returned and respectfully handed him a neatly folded package and a cup of hot water.

Tangar took the package, handed it caringly to Chilbain, and busied himself preparing a cup of tea using the gift he had brought. When the brew was ready, he gestured for Chilbain to follow him to the central hearth. The attending nurse followed with most of the women of the village in tow.

Holding the cup up to the sun, he called out in a clear voice. "Hail YodHeaVau. Whisper ever gently on his soul. We humbly ask Your blessing for this child – Chilcoat, his mother – Catherin, and his father – Chilbain. May they each know Your gift of a life well spent."

Gesturing to the package, he spoke to Chilbain. "Put it on the fire and drink this." He held the cup out to him.

Chilbain looked perplexed but followed the instructions. The packet hissed slightly as the flames began to consume it. A trail of smoke rose into the morning air as he sipped at the cup cautiously. "Eh... What is this? It's bitter."

"Of course it is. Drink up, and throw the dregs onto the flame. It must join the spirit of the mother's travail."

By the time he had choked down the last gulp of tea the smoldering packet had nearly vanished into the embers. He tossed the remaining mouthful of sediment in. It hissed and sputtered for a moment as the crowd of women began to break up, chattering approvingly at the display.

Chilbain turned to his friend. "Thanks, I guess. What was that all about?"

"I told you, homage to the mother. It's from the old ways."

"The old ways... Why do I think this was more for Molar's benefit than mine?"

"It was for all of us. You saw those women. They liked it. It recognizes them as special."

"Just the same, I don't think Molar's going to be happy."

"No. I suppose not, but I don't care. I think it's time that Molar finds his rightful place."

"And where is that?"

"Not here, not now. I've been talking with my dad and I need to go see Stafon and Talbot. He said some things that I want to get straight."

"Your dad? You're taking advice from him? I mean, are you sure that's a good idea? He doesn't make a lot of sense lately."

"That's just it. I think Stanton poisoned him. I mean, he was fine until we went to the gathering a couple of years back. He got into an argument with Stanton about the old ways and, before the meeting was over, Dad was sick. He hasn't been the same since. I think they poisoned him."

"Whoa... That's a pretty big claim. You got any proof?"

"No, of course not. They're treacherous cowards, but they're not sloppy. Just because there is no evidence, doesn't mean it didn't happen."

Pulling his hunting cloak over his shoulders, Tangar kissed Tarann on the forehead. "I'm going up by the falls. I should be back before dark. Molar has me on a goose chase looking for conch berries. He knows there are none up at the falls, but he wants me to go looking, just the same."

"Why? I mean, if he knows there are no berries up there, why send you?"

"I think he's punishing me for celebrating the birth in the old way. He wants me to refuse so he can report me to the council. He thinks he can replace me if I'm defiant."

"Can he do that?"

"If he can convince the high council but, right now, Bishain still has control so it's not likely."

"Why does he hate you so?"

"He doesn't hate me. He fears me and wants me out of the way so he can teach the enlightened path unchallenged."

"How much teaching can he do in one day?"

"I think he's going after the children. They'll not question him and, little-by-little, they'll get their parents to accept what he says."

"Is that bad? I mean, what can he say that will make any difference?"

"I don't know. He's going to say that his way is better and that everyone should recognize that."

"And how is that different from what you say?"

"But my ways, the old ways, **are** better. They've served us for generations. They don't need to be changed."

"Says you... I don't think you're going to convince anyone with that argument. I mean, after all, his way is easier. Everyone works together and everyone benefits the same. It's fair."

"Fair huh? You work hard for what you earn. Can you say the same for Benton or Maron? They're both layabouts that claim they've done more than they have. Do they deserve a fair share of your produce?"

"No. They don't deserve it, but they get what they need. Am I to deny them their needs?"

"You deny them the dignity of earning their keep."

"I deny them nothing. They find dignity in serving Molar's ways."

"That's not dignity, that's deception. Only their peers in the enlightenment praise them. Molar gives them menial tasks, producing nothing but proof of their servitude, and they think they're clever for getting away with it. It's more important for them to feel they've been clever than to actually accomplish anything. They take great pride in being witty about their deception."

"Speaking of menial tasks, you had better get going if you're going to get back before dark."

Tangar clinched his spear and realized that she was right. He too was serving Molar in a blatant display of submission. As he neared the edge of the village, he noted three of the elders sitting in the shade outside their lodge. *I wonder how Dad's doing. Perhaps he can give meaning to this task.*

"Dad, come with me on a walk. We'll go around the lake. That should be fun."

"Walking has long ago stopped being fun. What troubles you son?"

Tangar smiled broadly. The warmth of their old relationship comforted him in ways he couldn't express. "Well, how about we take a boat then?"

"Deep water..." Thoma looked concerned at the prospect and then seemed to lose focus as he ran his thumb along the length of his story wand.

"OK, we'll stay close to shore."

Tangar strained against the paddle as they finally neared the falls. The water cascaded down the cliff face and churned the lake to froth. The mist felt good on his face. "We made pretty good time considering the heat. It's a bit hot for this early in the season."

Thoma held his hand up and squinted at the sun. "Hea whispers of His discontent. He courts Vau with promises of change... The water's still cold."

His departure concerned Tangar. "Yeah, it's been a long winter. How about we put ashore here for a little while? I need to check on something."

"Laughing spirit." He gestured at the tumult of water pouring down the cliff as they pulled the boat ashore.

"Yeah... I need to look for some conch berries. I'll be right back."

"Fool's errand, there are no berries here."

"I know. Molar is testing my loyalty."

"Loyal to a fool?"

"Well, no. I'm just trying to stay on his good side until the council gives me your robes."

"You want them, take them…" Thoma turned his attention to his talking wand again.

Tangar made his way past the falls and stood on the cliff overlooking the lake. His father's words burned in his thoughts. *"Take them."*

If only it were that easy… Maybe Chilbain has the right idea. Maybe I should give Molar some of his own medicine. Maybe a little something extra in his tea, perhaps some banton root. That would serve him right for his butchery of the Blain girl. That poor child did nothing to deserve such treatment. He called boldly to the sky. "Hail YodHeaVau. Whisper ever gently on her soul."

Even those words concern me. What did Dad mean 'Hea whispers'? I've never heard him speak of just Hea in this way. Hea, is the god of lifeless things: the sun, the moon, and the stars. What could he mean that He courts Vau with changes? What changes could the god of lifeless things want? Surely, He doesn't want the earth to also be lifeless. Vau would never stand for such a thing. This is Her womb from which She brings forth the cycle of life. Surely, Dad is mistaken or has, again, lost his way.

Quickly scanning the meadow, he confirmed that no conch berries were there. He circled the pond feeding the falls and rested in the shade of an oak watching the birds in the meadow. Pulling an arrow to the ready, he soon dispatched a cock that had grown too bold about his presence. He bled the bird into a refreshing drink and was about to leave when he noticed a wollen tree near the cliff's edge. Quickly peeling some bark, he stuffed it into his pack along with the bird and headed back to the beach where he had left his father.

Tangar proudly dropped the bird carcass at his father's feet. "I got a bird and some wollen so this trip wasn't a complete loss."

Thoma looked up from the drawings he had carefully etched into the sand but didn't seem to notice the bird. He pointed at the circles and stones he had placed. "Hail YodHeaVau. The Spirit laughs with you."

Tangar scanned the symbol and noted Thoma's talking stick and several other twigs and stone thoughtfully placed. "Yes. I see you've been praying for us in the old way. You had better be careful doing that. The enlightened have forbidden it."

"Man cannot forbid God. He will be known to all who seek."

Tangar rattled about putting his gear back in the boat and nudged it into the water. "Hmm, yes, well, come along. Don't forget your stick."

As they glided slowly across the lake, Thoma scanned the shoreline and worried his talking wand as if remembering various stories that matched both themes. Tangar pulled easily on the paddle and watched the process silently, not wanting to interrupt his reflections.

At last Thoma spoke. "The time foretold draws near. Your children bear the burden of much sorrow."

"You can tell that from your wand?"

"I can tell that from your plight. You don't talk to me as you should. Am I so changed that you can't speak freely?"

"I'm sorry. I don't mean to be distant. I just can't tell when you..."

"When I am me... It's difficult for me also. At times, I can be who I am and at others, I'm lost to the spirit of enlightenment. I'm afraid my time draws near."

"Don't talk of such things."

"It's as it should be. I'm not afraid of dying... I'm only afraid I've left things undone; important things that need attention. Things that you need to know." He held his stick up as if offering it to him.

"Is there something on your wand that I don't already know?"

"There are many things you don't yet know. Be a loyal fool, look to the scrolls, and follow the Spirit's wands. You'll learn of things unimagined. Burdens of the children."

"Burdens? You keep saying that. What burdens?"

Thoma considered his words carefully and gestured with his wand toward the sun. "Hea whispers of a new world, for Vau will yield to His courtship. The children of Yod will be born anew from the burdens foretold."

Tangar stopped paddling and puzzled over his father's apparent loss of focus. *These are the times that are hardest for me. I know the old guy thinks he's making sense, but I just can't follow him.* "OK – I guess I need to reread the scrolls. I didn't find anything like that in them."

Thoma looked up as if just recognizing him. "Listen carefully for Hea whispers."

Tangar sat by the evening fire grinding the wollen bark into a fine powder. *I'm surprised at how little it makes when it's ground up this way. I'll need to go get more.* "... It just upsets me sometimes. He's so normal for a while and then he just seems to drift away. He said I need to reread the sacred scrolls."

"That'll be a little hard won't it? I mean, they're at the gathering village aren't they?"

"Yeah, and that's one damn long walk just to read a bunch of fairytales. I mean, I've already read them, and I don't remember anything like what he was talking about. He claims our children will understand because they're going to have to live through it."

"Our children? We don't have any children and it doesn't seem that we ever will." Tarann looked solemnly at the jumper she was sewing for Chilcoat.

"Oh, don't worry. Remember, Dad said we'll have a son and a daughter. He is 'the man foretold' and she is to be 'the keeper of the way' and mother of a new world."

"Don't! Don't wish such nonsense on my children. I just want a nice normal baby, not some witchcraft mumbo-jumbo."

"That's what I mean. It's really hard to talk with him anymore... He talked about dying. How is a son to speak with his father about dying? I wanted to push him into the lake."

"I'm sure he doesn't mean to upset you. He just says what comes into his head."

"That's just it. He shouldn't be thinking of such things. It's not good for him."

Tarann tugged her sewing into shape. "Can a son tell his father what to think?"

"He can if he knows better. I mean, he should be thinking about here, and now, not about dying, for God's sake."

"Maybe he is, when he 'drifts off', as you say. Maybe then he's thinking of good times and people he loves."

"Maybe – maybe I shouldn't talk to him. Maybe then he wouldn't think of such things."

"No. You need to talk with him, for your sake, if not for his."

"In the meantime, I need to figure out how to help the Blain girl. Molar's butchery needs attention. This wollen bark gave me an idea. If I can make a dressing to fit her leg and fill it with wollen, I think it will ease the pain, and over time, she can maybe learn to walk. I just need to get past her folks long enough to talk with her."

"I'll tell her mother that I need to measure her for a boot to help her walk. No mother could refuse help for her child."

"I'll get to work on it right away."

"Oh, please. Stick with the things you know how to do. I'll make the boot. You make your witches brew. Make it smell good. Barb will like that."

***

Tarann approached the Blain hut respectfully. "How are you? I've come to check up on Barb. I've been asked to see if I can help her get back on her feet."

"No! You can't. You and your husband have done enough. Can't you see we don't need your kind of help?" She gestured at her daughter fitfully tossing on her sleeping mat.

"Hello Barb. How are feeling?" Tarann tried to evade her mother.

The girl peeked from behind a tangle of darkened hair plastered to her sweaty forehead. "Not so good. It really hurts."

"Yes. I'm so sorry. I think maybe we can help you a little if your mother will let us."

"No! I told you. We don't want your help."

"Mom... Let her... I have to do something. I can't just lie here."

Tarann sidestepped her mother and moved closer to Barb. "Let me see how you're doing." She pulled the blanket up and noted the redness of her leg. "Hmm, yes. I think you're going to be OK as soon as we change that dressing and get you on your feet."

"You leave her alone. Molar put that dressing on this morning. He knows what's best."

"Molar is a busy man. He wants me to tend to this." Tarann hated to lie, but she knew infection when she saw it. Pulling a string from her bag, she quickly went about measuring her leg and cautiously peeked under the dressing wrap.

"I'll be back in a few minutes. I need to get a few things." She smiled reassuringly at Barb and respectfully bowed to her mother as she left.

When she returned, Tangar followed carrying various sticks and braces that appeared too awkward for Tarann to carry.

"What is all of this?" Mrs. Blain blocked the doorway.

Tarann moved to get past her. "It's just some things to be sure her leg doesn't get infected."

Tangar fumbled with the clattering collection of sticks more as a distraction than any real difficulty. He eventually bungled the load and scattered pieces across the floor toward Barb's bed. "Oops. Sorry. Here let me get that." He quickly crossed the room and knelt next to Barb long enough to assess the extent of her infection.

Collecting the wayward splints, he rose solemnly and turned to her mother. "Mrs. Blain, your daughter's leg is infected. I need to treat her right away."

"You've done enough. You're the reason she's here. Get out! Molar is treating her just fine."

He yanked the covers back exposing her swollen red flesh. "Here, look at this. Does this look like she's fine? You need to let me treat her."

Tarann moved to put her arm around Mrs. Blain. "Please. As a mother, you have to let him try to help. Don't let Molar bully you into hurting her. He's done things here that he shouldn't have. Please let my husband try to help."

"Please Mom. It really hurts." Barb squeezed her leg trying to stop the pain.

Mrs. Blain looked in anguish at her child. Tears welled in her eyes until she couldn't see. "Alright, but if she doesn't get better, I'm going to – I'm going to – kill you."

Tangar nodded acknowledgement to her with a slight smile. "That's fair. Now, please get me three cups of boiling water."

He quickly went to work mixing some muddy brown tea. "Here, drink this. It'll lessen the pain."

Removing the bandage, he scowled at the ragged flesh still dangling from the wound. "Molar truly is a butcher. I'm going to have to remove some of this flesh. It shouldn't hurt, but it will smell."

He dug into his bag and extracted a cup of slave that he spread liberally on the damaged flesh. Barb winced at his touch and squeezed her leg even harder. He took one of the splints of wood he had brought and stabbed it into the fire. The sparks rose through the chimney flap and he muttered. "Hail YodHeaVau. Please whisper ever gently on her soul."

When the potion had dulled the pain, he pulled the stick from the fire and waved it quickly to extinguish the flame. He examined it closely and blew gently on the smoldering embers. "OK. Here we go. Think of running again in the high meadow. Remember how the bees flee from your path as the flowers swim past you. What kind of flowers are they? Do you know?"

He held her leg and gently pressed the glowing ember to her flesh. It sizzled as a trail of smoke rose past his face. He pulled the stick away and struck it on the hearthstone breaking away the loose ash. The glow returned as he again blew gently on the ember.

"You're doing great. Are there any butterflies up in the meadow? Which is your favorite? What colors are they?" He repeated the process several more times until the stump of her leg was smooth and scabbed over with charred flesh. He applied a liberal coating of ointment and covered the wound with a new wrap.

He handed the packet of herbs to Mrs. Blain. "Here, mix a pinch of this with a cup of warm water when she's in pain. Be very careful. Don't use too much and not more than four times a day. I'll be back later to check up on her. Keep her cool with damp cloths and send for me if she can't be awakened."

"What am I to do with this boiling water?"

"Make some tea and pray that all goes well."

Tangar grabbed his weapons and started for their door.

Tarann tugged on his arm. "Are you sure that's a good idea?"

"No. I'm not sure of anything anymore. I have to face Molar and he probably has Lambert with him, so what am I to do?"

"Face him then, but weapons among tribesmen are never a good idea."

He considered his dilemma and put his weapons aside. "Alright, have it your way. But if Lambert puts a lance through me, you're going to have to find a new husband."

"No problem. Maybe I can find one that gets along with the neighbors."

"Yeah, and be sure he likes pulling weeds." Grabbing his medicine bag, he headed out across the village commons. He quickly checked in on Barb and noted that she slept quietly. Exchanging timid greetings with her mother, he proceeded to Molar's hut.

As expected, Lambert was sitting in the open doorway drinking a cup of wine and playing some sort of keep-away game with Maron, one of Molar's attending maidens. He had her hairpin and held it at arm's length away from her struggling grasp.

"I see you've found something constructive to do with your time."

Lambert ceased his game and looked at Tangar. Maron grabbed her comb and fled, tugging her dress back into order. "You should talk. Where's my conch berries?"

"Where's Molar? I need to tell him something."

"He's busy. Come back in the morning with the rest of the peasants. He might give you an audience then."

Tangar ignored his taunt and stepped through the door. Lambert tried to stop him, but he quickly dodged his drunken assault and stood in the middle of the room. Molar lay comatose on a pile of rugs in the corner. He had obviously consumed a great deal of the torish-root and had no concept of reality.

Tangar nudged him sharply with his foot. "Wake up you old fool! I have something to tell you. Wake up. Wake up."

"I told you to leave him alone." Lambert stood unsteadily in the doorway holding his spear at the ready.

"OK. Then you tell him I've tended to the Blain girl and I want him to stay away from her. She nearly died because of him and I'll not stand for it. If he has a problem with me, he should face me, not butcher an innocent child."

"Big talk while a man sleeps."

"He's not asleep. He's drugged up like all of the rest of the enlightened-few. Look... He hears me. He just can't figure out what I'm saying." Tangar took Molar's face in his hands and twisted it back and forth to expose his drooping eyelids.

Lambert assessed his boss. "That's enough. Get out. He'll tend to you when he's rested."

Tangar scoffed, picked up a half-full cup of cold torish tea and dumped it on Molar's head. "Wake up and listen to me!"

Molar groaned and attempted to sit up. The tea trickled down his face from the tangled mop of dirty wet hair. He squinted past the sting of the liquid. "You soil my spirit walk."

"I'll do more than upset your tea party. I've treated the Blain girl. You nearly killed her. I don't want you to go anywhere near her again. Do you hear me? Do you understand?"

Molar rubbed his face and squinted at the apparition before him. He wasn't sure if what he was seeing was real or imagined, but he knew he wasn't happy. "Go away. I don't want you here."

He attempted to lie down but Tangar grabbed him by the hair and pulled his head around to face him. "Listen to me. Do you understand me? I don't want you to ever do anything like that again, or I'll – I'll kill you."

Lambert sobered up enough to step in and jab his spear at Tangar's chest. "That's enough! Get out of here or I'll be the one doing the killing."

"Fine, you just make sure this pretender gets my message. I am Tangar, son of Thoma, the rightful Seer of the lakeshore tribe. I'll not stand for anymore of his hurtful stupidity."

***

Tarann listened intently to his story. "No. I'm not happy that you confronted him like that. We're going to have to move. There are people here that like Molar. Well, OK they respect him, or at least they respect the office. The point is; they'll support him, out of fear and intimidation from their neighbors."

"I know. Don't you think I've thought about all of that? It's just, well, you saw Barb. I can't just stand by and let him do that."

"I know. It's just – going to be hard. People don't like uncertainty. There are many that would rather have a bad Seer than an untested one. It's more – comfortable."

"Their comfort isn't my concern. Their health is my concern. Maybe a little discomfort would be a good thing. Dad said a time of much sorrow draws near. Maybe he's right. Maybe we should be preparing for the troubles foretold. Whatever that is... God I wish he could lead the people again. Things were so much better when he... Oh, never mind. I'm living in the past. It's not healthy."

"Troubles, sorrow, burdens foretold – maybe your father isn't correct. I mean, you said you didn't see such things in the scrolls. Maybe he imagines the troubles from a bad dream or a spirit walk with poison herbs."

"I know... That's what bothers me. If only he could read the scrolls with me. He could show me where he sees these things."

"Next year at the gathering, you can take him with you and read them together."

"Maybe, but he's so hard to talk with. Reading would be impossible. **That's** what bothers me. He's just not the man I grew up with."

"No, I suppose not. No one is. Maybe you should pray for his health. Maybe Vau will heal him enough to read with you."

"I have… I pray for him every time I see him. I'm afraid Vau has done all She can with the shell She's left him. The poisons have scarred him too deeply for Her mercy."

"I don't think that's possible. She can heal the dead. Isn't that what the scrolls say?"

"Of course, you're right. But, that puts the burden back on me. My prayers go unanswered. Am I not doing it correctly? Am I not worthy? Is there some plea I'm not making?"

"You know there is only one prayer that God will listen to. Speak from your heart and know that He hears."

"Hail YodHeaVau. Whisper ever gently on his soul."

The summer was nearly spent when Stafon appeared at Tangar's door. "Stafon, what are you doing here? It's good to see you. Come in. Come in. Tarann, please get us some tea."

"Tarann, how are you? You look good. I hope this tyrant has been treating you well. Laura says hello. She wanted to come, but I talked her out of it. She's three months pregnant now."

Tarann stoically served two cups of tea. "I'm fine. Tell her congratulations and I hope she stays well."

"Thanks. I take it that you don't have any news for her."

"No." She looked solemnly to Tangar for a moment and went back to the boot she was working on.

Stafon felt the edge in her voice and turned to Tangar. "Actually, I came to talk with you. I've been having a little trouble remembering some of the things in the scrolls. I mean, some of that stuff was pretty weird. I think I must be remembering it wrong or something. I figured since I was in the neighborhood, I'd stop by and see how you're doing with it."

"In the neighborhood? That's one damn long walk to discuss vagaries."

"Yeah, well, it's more a mission of mercy... I brought a couple of our young people that are having a hard time. Their folks died in an accident and I figured the change in scenery would do them good. Their mother was swept off the rocks by a wave and their father tried to save her. Ever since, the girls won't go near the water and that doesn't work out very well for fishing. Maybe you can find them something to do to take their minds off it. They'll probably recover in a few months and want to come home."

"Sure. How old are they? We can always use help in the fields."

"A couple of young girls; sisters. The eldest is nearly of age. I hope they can find comfort here. Maybe they can serve the elders for a while."

"We'll find something for them. In the meantime, I talked with my dad about the scrolls and he said there's all sorts of things in there that I don't remember."

"Yeah? How is the old boy? I'd like to hear what he has to say."

"He's as good as can be expected, I guess. We can try talking with him, but don't expect too much. He lives in his head a lot lately."

"Don't we all? Let's go see him."

The pair wandered casually across the village commons. "Sorry if I caused any trouble back there. I was just trying to make conversation."

"It's OK. She's just sensitive about babies right now. Say, I have to check in on a patient. You should come. It'll help you understand what I'm up against here."

Stafon stood somberly by as Tangar dressed Barb's wound. She was awake and in good spirits. "OK. Everything looks good. I'll be back later with some more medicine. You stay in bed. I don't want you running around getting into trouble."

She was intrigued by the presence of a stranger and smiled timidly adjusting the cover on her legs to expose a provocative flash of skin.

As the pair again walked among the village folks heading toward the elders lodge Stafon spoke quietly. "She's very – interesting. What happened to her?"

"She got a thorn. I pulled it out, but Molar decided that she needed more done and cut her foot off."

"A thorn for God's sake... Why didn't you stop him?"

"He sent me away to hunt herbs for him then decided it needed to be done."

"That seems kind of radical for a thorn. I mean, what happened that she needed that done?"

"I don't know. He claimed it was necessary and invoked divine knowledge of the enlightened-few. It was too late by the time I got back, and now I'm just trying to fix his butchery."

"What's enlightenment got to do with it?"

"Nothing as far as I can tell… He falls back on the political power of the 'new path' whenever he does anything corrupt. I think he wants her as a temple maiden, dependant on his drugs, and willing to do anything to get them. He has followers here that like the new ways and support him, so it's not easy to oppose him. I threatened him and he's kept his distance since, but as soon as he runs out of his torish tea, he'll probably get up the nerve to challenge me."

"Hmm, yes, we have the same thing at the western village, though we don't have Molar chopping people's feet off. What's your dad got to say about it?"

"I don't know if he even knows about it. As I said, he lives in his head a lot."

"Let's go ask him."

The pair soon stood in the elders lodge. The two young girls that came with Stafon were busy tending to a large woman that was having a great deal of difficulty standing up. Another, more experienced, girl was supervising them and seemed contemptuous of their effort. Thoma sat in his usual corner sketching prayer circles on the floor.

Tangar approached with concern that he would so blatantly exhibit the symbols of the past. "Hey Pop. How are you? I brought an old friend to see you."

Thoma peeked out from behind his bristle of tangled hair to scan the pair and casually reached to take a seashell from his nearby collection of trinkets. He squinted at Stafon for a moment as if trying to assess him then placed the shell thoughtfully near the juncture of two lines he had etched into the hard packed clay. "Friend indeed."

Stafon watched the placement closely. Other tokens on the board included his talking wand and two matching stones that probably represented Tangar and Tarann. "Hey old man. How are you? They keeping you out of trouble? I see you put me into Vau's clutches... You're probably right. I need to work on that."

Tangar looked guardedly at the seemingly busy senior attendant and studied the various pieces laid out on the figure. "Are you praying for us? Who are these others pieces?" He gestured at a small broken twig and two gray stones that were clustered together deep in Hea's arms.

Thoma scanned the figure and adjusted the position of a couple of pieces. "Those of concern... The child's pain weighs heavily."

Tangar glanced at Stafon. "Yes, I see... Then you know of her?"

"I am old, not dead. You treat the child, but not the others." He gestured at the cluster of icons.

"I pray as you do, but I get no answer. Am I to take revenge for the innocent?"

"You dwell too long in the arms of Vau." He moved one of the smooth stones deep into an arc of the symbol. "You must treat the sick for the ailments they suffer." He moved the cluster of gray stones into the same area.

"And what is the cure for stupid?"

Thoma looked disappointed at his son's stubbornness. "Knowledge, knowledge of the correct path."

Stafon snickered at the old man's resolve. "Say, speaking of correct paths... I was wondering if you remember in the scrolls where they talk about floating among the clouds."

"Of course, the Shanare do many wondrous things." Thoma noticed the supervisor girl was now watching them. He quickly drew a cloth over the symbol and moved to conceal the collection of prayer icons.

Tangar puzzled over his actions and glanced around to discover what had bothered him. "Is something wrong?"

Thoma picked up his talking wand and began worrying its contours. "A great many things are wrong." He gestured at the cloth he had spread. "The old ways disturb those that won't see."

Stafon gave the young girl an inquisitive glance. "Hmm, yes. Why is it that the enlightened-few want to be rid of the scrolls? What do they see in them that need be destroyed?"

The old man scoffed. "Truth – truth for which they have no appetite. It can't be explained without calling on the Spirit and that takes from the power they crave. They use His name freely, too freely, but they have no faith in Him. They have no room for faith in anything but their own power."

Stafon kept the girl in the corner of his eye. "The young are so easily swayed."

Tangar turned away from the girl. "The enlightened seek out the young. They are vulnerable to grand ideas without form or function. Ideas that are a panacea for all of the imagined ills contrived by the few. Any that questions their ideas quickly fall out of favor and no longer receive the warmth of their community. It's a very powerful force for the young."

Stafon watched the older girl leave and smiled approval to the two youngsters he had brought. "I came only to deliver my wards and clarify what is written, not to confront veiled threats and political unrest."

Thoma sorted through his cache of trinkets and pulled out his pipe. "The blanket of time warms what's written. Hold the scrolls lost for the Keeper shall bring forth the One."

Stafon offered the old man his herb pouch. "Now, see that's the kind of stuff in the scrolls that I don't understand. Who is this 'Keeper' and why should the scrolls be lost to him?"

Thoma measured a small pinch of herb into his pipe and lit it. Through the cloud of smoke, he nodded thoughtfully to Stafon. "Yes, you must hold the knowledge of the one."

Tangar shook his head slowly. "Well, I think that's enough for today. Pop, you try to get some rest. We'll stop by and see you again tomorrow."

Thoma tapped his empty pipe on his wrist. "Tomorrow the gathering. Momma calls me home... It will be good to see her again."

Tangar reflected on the loss of his mother. It had been years since she had died and it was comforting to see that his father still thought warmly of her. *Perhaps Tarann is right. Perhaps the times that Dad is lost in thought, he is thinking of her.* "OK, you get some rest. We'll talk about the gathering later."

As the pair left the elders lodge, Tangar spoke solemnly. "The gathering has also been in my thoughts. I fear the time has come to leave Dad at the northern village. They know how to care for the elderly until the end. Some of his old friends are already there, but I've resisted leaving him. It's just too cold, too final. He deserves more than just being abandoned to strangers. I've resisted as long as I can, but it's getting too hard, too hard to take care of him, too hard to face him."

Stafon put his arm over Tangar's shoulder as they made their way across the village commons. "That's a tough one. I don't know how you do it. I mean, he had a lot of good information, but he's just not the man I knew. Is that what's in store for us? I mean, if we become Seers, is that what'll happen to us? We eat too many herbs, drink too much spirit-tea, and just sort of drift off into our heads?"

"I don't think so. I think those bastards of the enlightenment poisoned him. He was OK until they came along and started trying to take over the council. He saw their scheme and tried to expose them, so they poisoned him. You can tell by the way they snicker behind his back. They think they have really pulled something and are proud of themselves. They revel in their power to do harm and get away with it."

"Hmm – and do you have any proof of this?"

"No, of course not."

"Have you asked your dad about it? Does he remember who did it, or what they did?"

"No. I don't think he knows. You saw him. He doesn't remember me half of the time, much less who spiked his tea two years ago. If he ever knew, he's chosen to forget it."

Tarann held a measurement string with marker threads dangling from it. "Get me an oak branch this long and this big around."

Tangar dropped the two rabbits he had killed and put his weapons away. "Oak... Are you sure you need oak? That means I'll have to go clear up by the falls."

"I think oak will wear best."

"Hmm – OK, but it's late, I'll have to spend the night. I'll see if Chilbain is up for it."

"Hmm, yes, you two stay out of trouble."

By late afternoon, the leisurely walk around the lake took the pair up the ridgeline to the high meadow. Tangar chopped away at a chosen branch while Chilbain prowled the meadow looking for a pheasant.

The pile of freshly cut oak twigs made a decent base for the fire as the pair relaxed at their evening meal.

"So how's fatherhood treating you?" Tangar placed the stump of the branch he had cut at the edge of the fire.

"OK, I guess. I don't do anything except hold him from time to time. He doesn't sleep much though. I mean, he sleeps all day and stays awake all night and he's very possessive of Cat. It seems like every time I try to get close to her, he wakes up and wants to eat."

"Sounds like you're jealous. Is he ready for the gathering? I mean, that's a long walk for one so young."

"Sure, I guess. Cat has it all figured out that we can trade off carrying him. It should be OK."

"Is she going to drag your cart while you carry him?"

"I have one of the Rancon boys lined up to help. It'll be slow, but I think we'll be alright. Are you guys ready?"

"Yeah, I don't know. Barb may need help so I'm going to stay close to the Blain's. That reminds me. I need to get some more wollen bark before we leave." He watched the steam rising from the oak stump and adjusted it closer to the embers.

"What about your dad? Is he ready?"

Tangar tugged at a frayed end of bark on the stump. "He says he is. He wants to stay on at the gathering. He says Mom is calling to him."

"Are you ready to do that?"

"Not really. I mean, I thought I could help him. You know, I thought if I could just take care of him for a while, he'd get better. But, it isn't happening. He seems to be getting worse, if anything… He got real paranoid about one of the caretaker girls when Stafon was here. He thought she was spying on him or something."

"Maybe she is. You never know with the enlightened-few. They have a way of creeping into things that you don't realize until it's too late."

"You sound as bad as him. Maybe you should stay on at the gathering village too."

"Say what you will, I don't trust those bastards to do anything without some hidden purpose. Look at Lambert. He's nothing but a drunken thug, yet Molar finds him worthy of office. His only qualification is his willingness to blindly obey without question."

"His willful ignorance provides him comfort; he isn't at fault for anything done. He's only doing as he's told."

"Can a man be so naive? He must see that Molar is using him."

"I think his willingness to follow the enlightenment is a sign of emptiness. He fools himself into believing his servitude makes him a man of distinction. He wants only to be accepted by the few who claim power."

Tangar peeled the bark away from the stump and tossed it onto the embers. Sparks scattered to the sky as he replaced it close to the hearth. Small beads of moisture collected along its length and quickly dried, leaving a dark residue. "Dad said I need to take his robes."

Chilbain tugged dryly on his pipe. "Sounds good to me. You can do it at the gathering. That way the council can bless it."

"Yeah, but that means I have to convince them I'm ready. God I hate politics… I'll have to meet with the council and answer a bunch of dumb questions. Some of the council are 'enlightened'. That means they'll ask stuff about the 'new way'. I may not be able to answer them."

"Sure you can. Just tell them you have 'awoken unto the light'. That's their answer for everything. That's all they want to hear. The enlightened path they're so proud of is nothing more than following orders of the few."

"I'm not sure I can do that."

"You don't have to. You just tell them you will, and then do whatever you want. That's what they do. They drink a bunch of spirit-tea, tell everyone that they speak only of righteousness, and then they sit around all day making up new rules to tighten their grip over us."

"Yeah – I just don't think I can lie like that."

"To them, it's not lying; it's the politics of the office. You do what you have to do to stay in power."

"How is that different from Lambert? An empty shell, doing the bidding of the few."

"It's a cost. Only you can decide if it's worth it."

"For now, it's too high. I need to talk with Bishain. If he'll back me, I can pull it off. Maybe I can get Dad to talk with him. They're old friends."

"Do you think your dad's up for that? I mean, that's pretty risky isn't it?"

"It could be. It all depends on how he's feeling. It could go real well, or it could be a complete bust."

***

Tarann sat cross-legged at the fire cutting strips of leather into long thin belts while Tangar crushed the wollen bark into a fine powder. "I hope this will be enough to get her through the winter. I guess it will have to be."

Tarann marked out places on the oak stump. "Here cut a notch here, here, and here for this belt to fit into."

The device had been smoothed and shaped into a fair approximation of an ankle. The foot itself was no more than a stub extending forward, but she figured future versions could be more elaborate if desired.

"Hmm – I'll need to sharpen my ax first. Cutting that branch really took a toll on the edge." He put the stump aside and fingered the stone thoughtfully.

"Well, do it outside. I don't want to step on one of your slivers again."

As he sat skillfully chipping flakes from the blade of his ax, his thoughts wandered to his father and his desire to stay on at the gathering village. *Maybe it would be a good thing. He would be well taken care of and perhaps less upset about being spied on. It just feels too soon. I'm not ready to let him go. In spite of his aimless conversations, I would miss his guidance, his wit, his knowledge. Maybe it's my weakness that I fear, not his. I just can't let go of him yet.*

Tarann skillfully bound the leather straps to the oak stub. The belts wrapped around the form catching the notches Tangar had cut. She had soaked the straps in brine and laced them snuggly into shape. Tangar had smoothed and stained the oak to match the leather and Tarann had trimmed and stitched the hide into a single uniform shape forming a remarkable bit of workmanship with the leather cup resting firmly on the end of the stump.

Tangar gathered the wollen powder on a piece of fine cloth and assessed his other medical supplies. He selected some dried rose petals and sniffed at their condition. *They make a soothing light tea that has the subtle fragrance of autumn.* He quickly ground them into a fine powder and mixed it with the wollen bark.

As he closed the packet of rose petals, he considered the guide stick used to secure the knot. It told of the path to the high meadow where the roses grow. *I'm not likely to forget that trail. Molar has me tending those plants religiously. The long slow process takes me away from home for weeks each autumn milking their 'blood'. Each seedpod needs to be scored just right to let its blood collect as a sticky brown gum that I have to harvest twice each day for weeks. It makes me sad. It seems cruel to starve the seeds in this way but the result is highly prized by all of the shamans. It is a painkiller unsurpassed by any other, but it is very dangerous. A small amount can kill if not handled correctly.*

Molar, himself, does the preparation. He greedily takes the ball of gum I harvest and dries it, grinds it, and mixes it with other herbs to fit his needs. I'm sure he would gather it himself if it didn't require so much work. He's not one to spend his energy on long walks and tedious labor.

The resulting powder is his main bargaining product each year at the gathering. Since the roses grow only in the highland meadows, the lakeshore Seer is responsible for the harvest. He holds it for ransom until the other shamans pay his bounty.

Tangar considered the small packet of rose-blood that dangled from the cord of the rose petals. He had used it sparingly when he first treated Barb, but she no longer needed such potent relief. *Adding a pinch to the wollen mixture would certainly guarantee that Barb would feel no pain but she's young, the pain is a part of her now. Perhaps it will serve to strengthen her in the ways of the world.*

Packing the wollen mixture into a soft leather pouch, he placed it next to the finished stump. "Can you stitch this cloth into a sock for her leg? It will comfort the fit and hold the medicine in place."

Tarann wrapped the cloth around the form she had been using and stitched a seam to close it into a tight contour. "We have to wait for the leather to dry but it should be ready tomorrow. Do you think she'll like it?"

"I'm not sure 'like' is the right word. I think she'll grow to tolerate it and perhaps, with time, she'll grow to appreciate it. I just hope it works well enough to allow her to make the trek to the gathering."

"If it doesn't work, well, maybe she can stay at the gathering village, then she wouldn't have to walk all the way back."

"Perhaps... Dad said that he wants to stay. Maybe she can stay to serve him there."

"Are you going to let him stay?"

"I'm not sure I can stop him. He's pretty obstinate on a good day. No telling what he'll get into his head by the time we get there."

The next day the pair gathered up the medicine and the stump and stood timidly at the Blain's door. "Hello Mrs. Blain. I'd like to see how Barb is doing."

"She's none of your concern now. Molar has seen to her and said we aren't to allow you near her."

"What? No! That can't be. I have something for her."

"We don't want any more of your meddling. Molar said..."

"Molar said what?"

"Great misfortune will befall us if we follow the old ways. He said we need to rid ourselves of the remnants of the past. He took my mother's necklace as penance to guard against the evil of the old ways. He said we'll only remain safe if we keep you away from her."

"I know this is a lot to ask, but you must fight against him. He cares nothing for Barb. He cares only for himself. Look at her; she's grown strong since I've been treating her in the old way. If he had treated her, she would be dead by now or worse, she would be a slave to his evil potions, forever bedridden, a servant to his wrongful ways. If you'll let me, I'll give her this boot to allow her to walk once again."

Tarann held the appliance out to her. "It's simply wood and leather, nothing wicked can posses it. You can make one like it or, perhaps, you can make a better one. See, it fits like a shoe to let her walk again. She'll soon be running and playing with her friends. If you'll let her."

"Mom, please – I don't want to be like this." Barb dumped the cup of tea Molar had provided.

"If I do this, the others will turn away from us. I'll have no friends."

Tangar hid the pouch of wollen powder behind him. "If some turn away, let them. They're not true friends; they're simply tools of the easy way. You'll then know who your real friends are and who are dupes of the enlightenment."

Tarann sorted out the long attachment straps and displayed the boot's design. "You'll have a whole daughter, able to work and live a full life, not a cripple, unfit for anything but Molar's temple maid."

Barb grabbed at the device and examined its structure. She immediately pulled her covers off and tried to fit the boot to her leg.

"Let me show you." Tangar stepped forward but hesitated looking at the shapely form of Barbs legs.

Barb looked pleadingly to her mother.

"Alright, if I'm to be shunned, let it be because I love my daughter."

Tangar took the sock from inside the boot and hesitated a moment before producing the satchel of wollen powder. "This powder will sooth some of the pain. Take a small pinch and dust the inside of the stocking before you put it on." He started to approach the young girl's naked leg but stopped and handed the stocking to her mother. "Here, you put it on."

She took the sock and sniffed at it expecting some foul stench of medicine. The faint aroma of the rose petals comforted her assessment.

Once the stocking was in place, Tarann took the boot and laid the straps out with one on either side of Barb's leg. Twisting the boot on, she wound the straps alternate up along her leg and finally around her waist where they were laced together.

Barb gazed at the contraption in disbelief. It didn't hurt as she had expected and it gave her leg a warrior-like appearance that pleased her.

Tangar held his hand out to her. "Try to stand up. Don't be afraid. Treat it as you would your own foot."

She stood unsteadily for a few steps and then let go of his hand and hobbled precariously across the room. The overly cautious limp soon brought her into her mother's arms. They kissed and cried for several moments as she teetered back and forth on her new leg.

Tangar smiled timidly and cinched the drawstring on the satchel of wollen powder. "Here, keep this dry and use it sparingly as I showed you. If the skin reddens or swells, stop using it and come see me. Wash your leg every evening and don't wear it at night until we see how well you adapt."

Mrs. Blain dried her cheek. "Thank you for all of this."

"Thank Tarann. She is the one that made it. I just followed her instructions."

In the weeks leading up to the gathering, Barb learned to walk with only the slightest limp and flaunted her 'special' foot by refusing to cover her leg in a flirtatious display of fashion sense. She became the envy of her friends. She could stand on her new foot on the hottest ground without discomfort and step on thorns without fear. Her prowess included spinning and dancing provocatively with newfound confidence.

She etched two snakeheads into the oak stump. Each merged with a strap wrapping up her leg and highlighted the nut-brown skin of her leg. This so impressed three of her girlfriends that they too started wrapping their legs with leather straps and refusing to cover them. This, in turn, inspired the young men of the tribe to wrap their arms in a like manner.

Such antics would normally not draw the attention of adults, but Tangar observed the miraculous healing power of her youth with delight while Molar showed a resentful awareness of the girl.

During the second week of the annual trek, Tangar resolved to let Barb deal with her malady in her own way. He had his hands full trying to keep his father moving. Every morning Thoma would refuse to get onto the cart and by midmorning, he would straggle behind so far that Tangar had to pull out of the traffic flow to let him catch up. Each day they had the same argument and, by afternoon, Thoma would eventually relent and climb aboard the cart to be "carried like a bag of dirty laundry."

As the gathering began, the striking new style of Barb and her friends caused restless stirrings among their peers in the other tribes. At first, it was simple astonishment but it soon transitioned to envy and mimicry. Barb had unwittingly set the style for the nubile youth for years to come.

Tangar approached the tent of the high council. "Talbot, it's good to see you. What have you been up to?"

"Oh, you know me, kissing up to Bishain and the guys. So how's it going with you? You have any kids yet?"

"Nah. I'm waiting for you to show me how. How about you, have you found a woman that'll put up with you?"

"I've been busy. Say, is Stafon going to show up this year? Have you heard anything from him?"

"Yeah, he came by a couple of months ago. He'll probably show. He had a lot of questions about the scrolls."

"Yeah, the lost scrolls... That's what I've been busy with."

"Lost? What do you mean – lost?"

"It's a long story. Let's get you settled first. Say, what's with the warrior princess you brought?" He gestured at Barb and her provocative band of followers.

"Ah, that's Barb. I'll introduce you. You might like her. She's a bit of a miracle. Molar cut her foot off, and she's come back like nothing ever happened."

"Whoa, why did he cut her foot off?"

"He claims she was infected, but I think he was just trying to make me look bad. We don't get along very well. Say, you're good buddies with Bishain… how about speaking to him for me? I'd like him to reassign Molar to somewhere else and let me takeover for the lakeshore tribe."

"Hmm – I'll get you a meeting, but you'll have to convince him yourself. I don't want that hanging over my head."

"I knew you could help. Now, come and say hi to Tarann. She'll be about ready to strangle me if I don't take Pop off her hands."

"How is the old boy? Still giving you a hard time?"

"Yeah, come on. He probably won't remember you, so don't be surprised. I'll introduce you."

The awkward walk across the jumble of partially erected tents and piles of household belongings brought them to his hut.

Talbot approached the obviously busy woman of the house. She had a shock of her red hair pulled back into a tight bun that he knew as her sign of low tolerance. "Tarann how are you? It's good to see you."

She looked up from her task and tried to put on an air of civility. "Talbot... I might have known you'd be keeping him from his chores... I'm sorry. Hi. I'm good. I'm glad to see you." She gave him a quick hug and whispered harshly to her husband. "Now, do something with your father before I do."

Tangar hugged her quickly. "Yes Dear. I was just about to do that. OK, hey Pop, you remember Talbot? We're going to take you to the elders lodge now. OK?"

Thoma sat dejectedly on a pile of rugs dropped in the middle of the floor. "Of course I remember him. He's the one that chants off key."

"Ha! That's me alright. How have you been? How would you like to go see Bishain? I'm sure he'd like to say hi."

"Yes, of course, of course. I need a gift. Yes, a gift..." Thoma's eyes glazed over as he thought of times gone by.

"You are gift enough. He wants only to speak with you again."

"To speak again... Yes, yes the time draws near."

Talbot extended his hand. "Great, come along then... Tarann, I'm sorry I have to leave so soon, but I have a mission."

A slight smile crossed her face as she remembered his persuasive ways. "It was good to see you. I'm sure we can get together later."

The meandering path around the jumble of partially erected tents took them past the elders' lodge. Molar sat under the terrace-cover amongst the other tribal leaders. They all drank lightheartedly from a common bowl of dusty gray tea. Lambert joked with his fellow guardians gathered at the base of the steps.

Thoma started to head toward their tent, but Talbot gently redirected him to the temple. "We'll stop by their later. Right now we should say hi to Bishain."

The trio entered the outer room of the high-temple and stood impatiently waiting their turn. Thoma dug into his pocket and extracted a small pouch of smoking herb. Tangar bordered on embarrassment by the gesture and Talbot seemed a bit uncomfortable.

At last, Nolan appeared in the doorway of the inner sanctum. He held the curtain back and bowed them into the room. Bishain sat on a throne-like pedestal covered in layers of carpet.

Thoma held his meager offering in the palm of his hand and offered it to Nolan.

Nolan looked questioningly to Talbot but took the offering with his fingertips and approached the high-elder timidly.

Bishain looked up from the text he read and focused on the humble packet held out to him. Taking the offering in his open palm, his look of confusion lost out to open glee as he focused on the trio standing before him.

The attending crowd of witnesses gasped in astonishment as the high-elder quickly descended the platform and fell to his knees at Thoma's feet. "Thoma – I beg your pardon."

Thoma seemed unsurprised by the assault and placed his hand gently on Bishain's bowed head. "All are as one. Bow no more."

Bishain quickly rose to his feet and waved to Nolan. "That will be all for now. Take these things and leave us."

Nolan gathered the pile of offerings and swept the remaining attendants out pulling the curtain closed behind them.

"Thoma old friend, I'm glad that you made it. Come, sit with me and tell me how you've been."

Nolan soon returned with a serving of light green tea and fruit. "Will there be anything else?"

"Yes, bring my rug... So, Talbot you manage to serve, despite your reluctance."

Talbot smiled meekly. "I gladly serve the One."

Nolan brought a neatly rolled carpet that he placed at Bishain's side and backed out of the room pulling the curtains closed.

Bishain gestured to the trio. "Please, eat, drink… Will Stafon be joining us?"

Talbot looked to Tangar. "I guess he hasn't made it yet. Perhaps tomorrow."

"Then we'll begin without him." Bishain sipped at his tea and called out. "Nolan, bring me some honey." He listened intently to be sure Nolan didn't respond. "Good, we're probably alone. Will you pray with me?" Several trinkets fell free as he unrolled the carpet and smoothed it into place in front of them.

The intricately woven sunburst design jumped at Tangar. "It's beautiful work. Who did this?"

"It is many generations old. Some say Vau Herself wove this tapestry to beguile Hea at the first joining. I think it's rather newer than that, but it is indeed a work of art."

The high-elder sorted the collection of bones, sticks, and stones that had fallen free. Thoughtfully selecting his favored icon, a small stone pyramid, he placed it in the center of the figure and then moved it slowly into Yod's realm. "I am."

He then took the pouch of smoking herb Thoma had offered and placed it in the center of the diagram.

Thoma watched the gesture with deep concern. He reached out to the figure and moved the pouch deep into the arms of Vau. "I am."

Bishain watched his friend's face closely as he performed his action. He then sorted through the collection of trinkets and selected three nearly identical, carved, rib bones. Each was adorned with a smooth rounded head and slightly curved body. "Our three novitiates play a role of concern."

He placed each figurine in the center of the diagram and then moved them one-by-one to the far edges of the sweeping arcs. "One in Yod, one in Hea, and one in Vau. I'll leave it up to you to decide who is who." He smiled slightly at Tangar's puzzled expression.

Tangar considered his role in the prayer. Quickly searching the remaining trinkets he noticed a smooth dark stone with a touch of red embedded in it. "If I'm to play this game of fools, I'll have Tarann with me." Scanning the field, he considered his situation and placed the stone next to the bone in the field of Hea. "I am."

Talbot grabbed a chubby round stone and a smaller version of the same object. "Since my brother Stafon is not here to defend himself, I'll place Laura and his child with him here in the arms of Vau. That leaves me alone in Yod." He nudged the final bone figurine to straighten it's view of the field. "I am."

Bishain looked solemnly at the collection of trinkets scattered across the tapestry. "And what concerns us then?"

Tangar took the opportunity to bring up his desire of ridding himself of Molar. Scanning the remaining icons, he selected two drab gray stones and placed them with him in the field of Hea. "Molar concerns me with his disregard for the wellbeing of the tribe. He thinks nothing of killing the innocent to satisfy his lust for power."

Bishain fingered one of the gray stones. "So is this the innocent of whom you speak?"

"No. That is Lambert, Molar's guardian."

"Then where is the innocent one?"

Tangar scanned the trinkets and picked a skinny little twig with a broken leg. "Here, here she is." He placed the twig in the cluster of trinkets he had collected near his icon.

"If she is innocent, as you say, does she belong there with you and these scoundrels?"

"No. I guess not." Tangar considered Barb and the troubles she had endured. He moved the twig into the warmth of Vau's arms.

Thoma clasped his hands and held them under his chin as he considered the field of prayer. He reached slowly out and picked up the twig. Holding to his chest for a moment, he placed it in the center segment of the diagram. "I know this child. Her warmth finds no blame in this concern."

Bishain scanned the figure. "Is this our only concern then?"

Tangar collected the two ugly gray stones. "This concern goes much deeper than these two. The concern is that the enlightenment preys on the weak minded. The people no longer feel the warmth of God. This concern can't be fixed with these few icons."

He dropped the stones on the figure and picked up a handful of loose trinkets from the pile and scattered them across the tapestry with a flamboyant wave of his hand. "These people care nothing for us or our prayer. There is no room for God in their world. They care only for themselves, and the new way. The awakening of the enlightenment promises them a fair share but gives them only servitude. It robs them of the nobility of meaningful work in exchange for blind obedience to the enlightened-few who revel in their deception and covet the cleverness of being idle."

Thoma seemed not to notice the theatrical gesture and carefully moved his packet of herbs closer toward the center of the diagram avoiding several of the wayward trinkets. "Keep that which is written from loss for the man foretold is born. The time draws near."

Bishain watched the transaction with great concern and moved his icon next to packet of herbs. "As you see."

Collecting the packet of herbs, he held it in his open palm for several moments as if he expected it to speak. Handing it back to Thoma, he rolled the tapestry into a neat bundle trapping the errant icons. He then rose to replace the bundle among the rugs collected in the corner. Moving several of the carpets aside, he pulled a neatly sewn package from the depths. He considered the parcel for a moment and held it out to Talbot. "Take these and find that of which we speak. Share their knowledge with your brothers and find the way foretold."

Talbot recognized the bundle as the sacred scrolls. "Is Nolan to tutor us again?"

"No. I'm afraid Nolan no longer serves our cause. You three each play a part in discovering the lost knowledge of the Shanare. No other will see what you shall see."

With Stafon's arrival, the trio again spent a great deal of time reading and rereading the scrolls. Tangar pulled fitfully on his pipe. "OK. I think I understand most of these two but this one is just gibberish. It's no wonder the enlightened want to get rid of them"

Stafon carefully unrolled another of the delicate scrolls. "Yeah, I wouldn't want to have to explain some of this stuff."

Talbot sat across the remote clearing they had chosen as their library. "That's too bad since that's exactly what we're supposed to do."

Tangar blew repeatedly though his pipe trying to clear it. "I don't know. I don't think so. I mean, it says right in this one that 'the one foretold' is the only one that can figure it all out. That's not us. At least, I don't think so. See here, *'he's the child of the Keeper'* and she's some kind of witch woman that's to *'know the way of suffering'*. Whatever that means..."

Stafon grumbled at the scroll he held. "That's just great. We need to fight against the power grab of the enlightenment and all we have is promises of witchcraft and endless suffering."

Talbot inched aside slightly trying to stay in the spot of shade he had selected. "Maybe you're right. Maybe our only job is to keep these things safe until the right time."

Tangar relit his pipe. "I don't like it. It's too passive. We need to do something now. I have Molar to deal with and all of this crap isn't getting that done."

Talbot tied the unruly document back into a neat roll. "No. I'm afraid your problem with Molar has everything to do with this. He and his kind are leeches sucking the life out of our people. The enlightenment is nothing more than an opportunity to hide their corruption behind 'awakening unto the light'."

Stafon also sought shade. "That's true... They find the awakening very – convenient. They cower behind their unity and claim that, what they do; they do 'for the children', 'for the betterment of all right-thinking people', 'for the people that are unable to do for themselves'. 'For only they understand the enlightened way'."

Tangar coughed and waved the smoke away from his face. "What a bunch of crap. They know nothing but their own greed."

Talbot tried to remain detached. "Perhaps, perhaps you're too harsh. Surely some of the people that follow the new way mean well."

Tangar tried in vain to relight his pipe. "They mean well, but they let themselves be led to slaughter. Look at what Molar did to Barb. Was that the act of a right-thinking man?"

Talbot rummaged through his pack. "We have only your word that he did wrong."

"You doubt my word?"

"Take it easy. I'm just saying, you weren't there. Her foot could've gotten infected, and he did the right thing."

"I know, but – I don't think so. She was fine when I left. I've treated thorns before. She should've been OK."

"But it's possible that she got worse."

"That's the problem with these people. They cultivate doubt like a prized flower. 'It's possible, so it must be allowed', even though it's unlikely. They conceal their corruption in the name of fairness. It's insidious."

Talbot stood at the edge of a puddle of sunlight that streamed through the surrounding trees neatly packing the four scrolls into their case. "Here we are, hiding the unforgivable sin of reading. Are we so pure? And, as for your issue with Molar, you're going to have to prove to the council that you're ready to assume the duties of the Seer. Your father is right. You need to play their game better than they do. If you want his robes, you need to take them."

Tangar clinched his spear. "There game of drinking spirit-tea and abusing the serving girls. I don't think I can do that. It does nothing for the people I serve."

Stafon gathered his weapons. "Then change the rules. Make them play your game. Wait until they've had their fill of tea and slip them some banton root. That should keep them busy for a while."

"Temping as that sounds, I need something more. Something that'll make them think, not just crap their guts out. I need something that will make them find in my favor."

"Yeah, well, good luck with that. The enlightened elders won't find in your favor no matter what you do. They'll do whatever Stanton wants without question. He knows you don't respect him and **that** is the unforgivable sin. Your only hope is that Bishain can hold sway."

Tangar turned to Talbot. "Speaking of which, how do you think it went with my dad? I mean, Bishain seemed to treat him like some kind of special dignitary. Does he do that for all of his old friends?"

"I've never seen it before. I mean, sure, he's respectful to all the old coots that come to visit, but I've never seen him so much as nod his head, much less bow to someone. There's more there than we're to know."

"Yeah, it was really weird. It didn't seem to surprise Dad though. He acted like it was totally normal... Really weird... He's talked about staying on here. I mean, there's not much left for him at the lake. He just sits around watching the plants grow and praying, and now, even that's causing trouble with a couple of the followers of the new way. They think he's causing dissention among the elders."

Stafon rattled his spear. "So? That's his job. If you can't stir things up when you're old when can you?"

Tangar shook his head trying not to laugh. "It's not that he's stirring things up, it's that he's started praying in the old way. He has the symbol etched into the floor and he just sits there and plays the game of fools. One of the attendants was upset by it, and that concerned him, so he included her in his prayer. That made her even more upset because she thought he was doing witchcraft on her. She doesn't understand and she doesn't want to learn. She wants only the comfort of the things she knows."

Stafon stepped onto the fallen log he had used as a bench. "That's the trouble with these people, they don't want to know. They don't understand that 'comfort' means you're not learning anything, you're just confirming what you already think. If you are to learn something, you shouldn't be comfortable with what you hear. It should upset you and make you think, not comfort you into complacency. They're happy that the enlightened-few deal with matters for them. They're happy to let that bunch of old sots sit around drinking and telling each other how superior they are as long as they don't have to deal with the obligations of real learning."

Talbot pulled the pack over his shoulder and turned to Tangar. "All this whining and complaining doesn't change anything. Nobody likes a whiner… It weakens your case and undermines your support for; you still don't wear the robes of the Seer."

Tangar planted the butt of his spear. "Nor do you. Are you without a challenger?"

"Bishain has trained me, and no other, to assume his duties. When he no longer wishes to perform, I'll step in."

Stafon used his spear to steady himself as he stepped down from the log. "The enlightened feel there is no need for training such as we have endured. They deny the spirit and the need for God while they use sacred herbs for pleasure rather than guidance. Do none of them challenge you?"

Talbot considered his answer. "There's Nolan, of course. He and some of his followers question my authority, but they're cowards that talk big only when they themselves are unchallenged. They have no beliefs to follow other than some vague crap about 'awakening unto the light'. Most of them don't even know what that means; they just repeat it because their friends nod and agree."

Stafon pulled his spear from the earth and cleaned the mud from it. "If enough agree, do they not rule the day?"

"So far, they agree only that they agree. They don't really know what they are agreeing to. They know only that it's comforting to join with their fellows."

Tangar pushed past his friends. "As you say, all of this complaining is getting us nowhere. I need to check up on Dad. I don't want him hanging around with that bunch of louts. They'll poison him again."

Talbot looked concerned. "Then you're not going to let him stay?"

"I don't know. I guess I'm just not ready to let him go yet. It all seems too – final. I mean, when the old come here to stay, they only live a few more years and then they're gone forever. I'm just not ready for that."

Stafon scoffed. "Do you think you can keep him alive by not letting him retire?"

"No. It's not like that. I know his days are few. I just want to be a part of them. I know he thinks the pain will be less for me if he stays here, but I'd rather feel his pain than loose him too soon."

Talbot adjusted his pack as the trio made their way back to the village. "Have you told him this?"

"Of course, but he only hears what he wants to hear."

"And is his son any different?"

"Of course I'm different. I hear you, I just find very little of value in what you say."

"And is your father any different?"

"Don't confuse me with facts. You know what I'm saying. I just want to protect him for as long as I can."

The trio slipped into the village by way of the western trail and soon stood near the elder's tent.

Talbot noticed the antics of a young girl dancing nearby. She was spinning dizzily on one leg for a small group of onlookers. Her flowing gown offered enticing glimpses of her form. "Say, isn't that the girl you treated?"

Tangar smirked at her exhibition. "Yeah, that's Barb. Come on I'll introduce you. She'll set you right."

Talbot broke his gaze and stammered. "I, I have to return these." He clutched at the pack of scrolls.

"Suit yourself, but you'll have to meet her someday. She's going to be your wife. It says so right here in the third scroll." Tangar poked at the treasure Talbot hid behind.

"It... She... You... Don't joke like that. You know it doesn't say anything of the sort. Besides, she's too young."

Stafon noted the awkwardness of their friend. "I don't know. She looks pretty good to me. Of course I'm an old married guy, with a pregnant wife I need to get home to, so any young girl looks good to me."

Talbot tried to salvage what little dignity he could. "Never mind that. I'm going to return these and talk with Bishain about some of what we read. Anyone want to join me?"

By now Barb had stopped dancing and stood glowing with energy as she instructed her friends on how she is able to do it. A couple tried to mimic her grace, but found their feet a hindrance. She looked up and smiled timidly at Tangar and his awkward friend.

Tangar waved and clapped silently for her. "Nah. I have to get home too. I need to go see how Dad's doing. Let me know if you figure anything out."

The games were in full swing and Stafon had again placed favorably in the spear throw.

Tangar avoided the competition in favor of time spent with his father. The energy of the gathering seemed to invigorate the old man. Just as in the old days, he regaled a small audience of youngsters with the stories that flowed from his talking wand. They gathered at his feet and fidgeted about while he softly stroked the crooked little twig. When they settled enough, he would select a particular bump or knot along its length and begin his story pointing to the blemish as if it alone knew the outcome of the tale.

A tear formed in Tangar's eye as he watched the wise old man retell story after story for his audience. There was no hesitation or faltering in his voice. The stories flowed from some deep archive of knowledge that even time and too many toxic potions couldn't diminish.

***

Thoma sat pensively at the evening fire in Tangar's tent. "Spirit dances..."

Tangar puzzled over the outburst for a moment and resolved that he was speaking of the ritual involving his collection of guide sticks. "Do you remember where you put them?"

"The woman took them."

The curt response stung his ears. He knew the old man called Tarann "the woman" when he was unhappy with her dominance of their domestic scene. It had been a particularly difficult trek this year, and both Tarann and Thoma were short of tolerance.

Tangar rummaged through the pile of carpets, clothes, and utensils that remained packed at the side of the tent. "Ah, I think I found it." He tugged at the tightly tied bundle and triumphantly placed it in his father's lap. Sitting back in his place, he looked expectantly at his father.

Thoma remained unmoved staring blankly at the package. Slowly placing one hand on it, he stroked it like a favored dog, but didn't move to open it. "The Blain girl is of fine spirit, very pretty."

Tangar feared that he had slipped, once again, into forgetfulness. "Yes, she is. Is there something else you need?"

"Do you think she'll bond this year?"

"I don't know. She's still young. She has time."

Thoma finally looked at the package in his lap as if for the first time. "Dance of knowledge."

Carefully unwrapping the medicine cloth, two bundles of neatly bound twigs fell free. He set them aside and spread the cloth on the floor. Smoothing the fabric into place, he scanned the blaze of yellow and red that transformed the drab brown cloth into a thing of beauty. The colors blended into a sunburst pattern that represented the northern village.

Tangar knew the cloth well. His father used it whenever he had a big decision to make. He spreads the fabric, just as now, and 'dances' with the spirit wands. That much is good and wholesome. It's what follows that he dreads. The dance culminates with the selection of a single guide stick that leads to a 'walk' with the chosen spirit. "Now wait a minute Pop. You aren't thinking about a spirit walk are you? You're not up to that kind of thing."

Thoma grabbed a bundle of twigs, untied them, and shook it at his son. "Wands speak wisdom. Listen carefully."

"You want me to spirit walk? I'm not sure I'm ready for that either."

"Spirit of understanding binds all."

"OK. Sure Pop, I know. But, it's not that easy, Molar..." He caught himself.

Thoma looked solemnly at his son, clinched the bundle firmly, and stirred it above the center of the diagram. "Hail Yod, child of Spirit."

Spreading the collection gently across the cloth, he pressed his open hand on them for a moment. "Hail Hea, father of all."

Once again collecting them into a bundle, he held them firmly to his chest. "Hail Vau, mother of life."

Raising them over his head, he dropped them onto the cloth. "Hail Yod. Gather knowledge."

They scattered randomly across the design and settled as an untidy heap. He focused on the jumble for a moment and removed those that crossed over the outer boarder of the design.

Collecting the remaining sticks, he inspected each before again clinching them as a bundle over the cloth and letting them fall. "Hail Hea. Whisper of change."

He sat for several moments assessing the pile of twigs. As he retrieved each outlier, he verified its identity and carefully set it aside with the other rejects. Taking note of the order in which he un-stacked the remaining jumble he, once again, collected them into a neat bundle.

He dropped them one last time and removed the outliers as before. "Hail Vau. Sing of life."

The few remaining twigs drew his attention as he once again assessed their pattern. Carefully selecting the topmost stick from the pile, he held it out to Tangar and spoke softly. "Hail YodHeaVau for this gift of wisdom."

Tangar hesitantly took the twig and gazed at its intricate kinks and bends. "Am I to find meaning in this?"

"As you will." He gathered all of the twigs and bundled them together, handing them to him. "My dance, my meaning."

"You mean you want me to dance with the wands?"

"Dance as you will... The Blain girl is very pretty." He gestured across the clearing to where she tended her family's dinner.

***

Tangar used the twig to illustrate his story. "... Then he handed me this stick. What am I supposed to make of that?"

Tarann listened dutifully and took the stick from him to show she was listening. "What's it for? Maybe that'll tell you what he's talking about."

"I think it's trancon. It's just one of his spirit herbs. I don't think it means anything. I think he's just making sure I know how to dance with the spirit wands. I mean, I've watched him do it a hundred times. What's new about this time?"

"So, what're you going to do with it? Don't you need it if you become Seer?"

The question struck him to the core, not that he cared about the stick, but that his wife would question his commitment of becoming the Seer. He took the twig back, turned it over thoughtfully for several moments, and finally replied. "Of course, I'll need it. I just wish I knew what he's trying to say. He's such a challenge sometimes... I mean, watching him with the children this morning was so warm and hopeful and then, this evening, with the sticks; it's just hard to see him this way."

"Do you still respect him?"

"Of course... What kind of a question is that?"

"Then follow his wisdom as you would."

"You're telling me to follow this guide stick and walk with the spirit my father has chosen for me."

"You said he told you to 'dance'. That sounds like you should pick your own stick."

Tangar considered his wife's wisdom. *She sees that which I can't, or won't. I'm perhaps too close to see clearly.* He stuffed the stick in with the others. "He didn't even use the right wands. These are for summer. They fit the lakeshore side of the cloth. They point to nothing I can reach for months."

As he took the second bundle and placed it next to the first, he scoffed. "These are the winter sticks. These are the ones that fit the temple side of the cloth."

He covered the bundles with the ends of the cloth and rolled it tightly into a package that he tied closed. "Right now I have Molar to contend with. There's talk that he's going to wed someone from our tribe. Do you know what that means? That means I can't claim that he's an outsider that's unfit to be the Seer."

"Who would have him? None of the women I know want anything to do with him."

"I don't know. Maybe one of the widows or someone that's been put out. I mean, the Seer's wife is a pretty good place politically."

"Still, who wants a layabout sot?"

"The price of power... Speaking of which, will you bond with me for another year?"

"You wait until the day before the ceremony to ask. I thought you were going turn me out because I haven't given you a son."

"Don't be silly. I would never turn you out. We'll have our son when the time is right. In the meantime, will you please bond with me?"

***

As the ceremony began, Barb proudly led the procession of the youngest girls along the path leading to the temple courtyard. She danced provocatively up the path, spinning from time-to-time on her wooden foot. The leather bands winding up her gracefully sculpted leg flashed playful into view. Her delicate form and confident manner belied her youth and drew the attention of many of the young men.

As she progressed toward the temple entrance, she hesitated for a moment, smiled, and bowed respectfully to Tangar. These antics were not unusual but they were normally reserved for clan elders or the tribal Seer in particular. Molar, of course, noticed the respect shown and bristled at the display.

As one of the youngest girls, Barb's turn soon came and she stepped proudly to the base of the women's knoll. She allowed her robe to part, boldly exposing the serpents winding up her leg. Her father stepped up beside her and spoke clearly. "As you can see, my daughter is not without blemish. She's a fine healthy spirit and will make a good wife but since this is only her first offering, I'll not see her wed to one too young. Her malady has seasoned her beyond her years and she needs a man who can cope with a strong will."

She held her head high, seeming to disregard her father's somber concern. She felt no need for his protective manner. The cluster of young men that had risen for consideration began to dwindle as the more timid assessed the competition.

She scanned the remaining contenders and shook her head in disappointment. She knew them all from years of friendship and none seemed worthy to her. Nolan, the prime elder, called for any others and was about to discharge her when Molar stepped forward. "I'll take care of her. She'll need my attention when that toy fails and her leg is once again infected."

The crowd fell silent at the prospect and the shock on Barb's face revealed her contempt for the idea. Everyone considered that perhaps he sees something of her future and knows that she'll soon be a burden on any mate she may take.

Molar recognized her disdain and tried to bolster his case. "When her youth begins to fail, she'll not be able to manage the pain. She'll need someone that can deal with her burden."

Barb shook her head rejecting the proposal, but her father tugged at her arm. "You must think of your future. This man can provide for you in ways that your mother and I can't. Will you at least consider him?"

Barb was near tears as she looked at Molar. *He's shamelessly smug. I hate him. How can they do this to me?* "No Poppa. No! I won't. Please, don't make me."

Molar attempted to put his arm around her shoulder. "Don't worry. I'll treat you well. I can take your pain. I have potions that will make you forget your loss."

She ducked away from his grasp, pulled the wreath from her hair, and threw it to the ground at his feet. "I don't want to forget! You did this to me. I want to remember every minute of pain. I want you to pay for what you've done."

"Oh child, yes I did this to you. I saved your life. I did what I had to do to stop the festering left by that fool Tangar. Don't you see? It was I that saved you, not him."

Tangar stood with Tarann wishing he had his spear to throw rather than garland. "That's enough. You can malign me all you want, but don't you dare try to take this girl against her will. Everyone knows that a simple thorn removal should not have ended with this. Even if it was infected, a drawing salve would've cured it. What you've done here you've done to spite me. You know it, and now everyone else knows it."

Talbot approached alongside Bishain. The two spoke quietly to each other for a moment and then Bishain turned to the crowd. "This is the gathering of souls. I'll not have it tainted with conflict."

Turning to Barb, he spoke softly. "I'm sorry Dear. You should not have to endure such strife. Talbot, stay with her."

He then took his scepter firmly in hand and pointed it first at Tangar and then at Molar. "You two come with me."

The three men solemnly retired to the high-elder's quarters. "Molar I am disappointed in you. You are a senior council member. You should not stoop to such childish behavior. I'll not stand for it."

He then turned to Tangar. "If you ever hope to assume your father's robes, you must learn to think of your people first. That poor girl has been through enough without you two turning it into some kind of cat fight."

Tangar clinched his fist. "This fool..."

Bishain held his scepter up in Tangar's face. "Silence! Wait your turn. Molar, what do you have to say of this?"

Molar smirked at the respect shown his position. "I feel responsible for what has happened to that poor girl. I let Tangar deal with a simple thorn removal, but he wasn't ready. She got infected and I had to step in before she died. I knew he was incompetent and I shouldn't have let him deal with it. Now, I want to help her get past this trouble. I'll take her as my wife, and tend to her needs."

"I see. And now, Tangar, what do you say of this?"

"The thorn removal was done correctly. She was well on her way to healing when Molar sent me away to fetch herbs for the spirit-tea he dinks for pleasure. By the time I returned, he had butchered her..."

"You're at fault, not I! You left the poisonous tip and it nearly killed her. You're the butcher. You don't know what you're doing and should never wear the robes of a Seer. Just like your father, you chant to the wind and play with sticks and stones. Well, I don't believe such nonsense. I believe in my years of experience and my knowledge of right and wrong. What you did was wrong and I did what I needed to do to correct it."

"You lie! You want only to take her..."

Bishain again swung his scepter. "Silence! Your outbursts don't help your case. If you have any facts that support what you say, I'll listen, otherwise don't waste my time."

Tangar clinched his jaw and tried to recall some detail that might help him. "It's plain to see that Molar has done this to undermine me as Seer of the lakeshore tribe. He unjustly criticizes me and plots to steal one of our young women against her will. He speaks ill of my father and the knowledge of the elders that has served our people for many generations..."

"I plot only to save our people from the misguided ignorance of the past. We must progress in the new way or we'll all suffer under..."

"You interrupt me and go un-scolded, yet each time I speak, I am chastised. This hearing is nothing more than..."

Bishain dropped his scepter to his side. "That's enough! This hearing is over. Molar you are to abide by the traditions of our people. If the young woman you have selected does not want your attention, then you are to forget her for this season. Perhaps in another year she will see wisdom in your proposal. Tangar, if you wish to pursue the robes of the Seer, you must prove your knowledge in all things, both new and old."

As the trio emerged from Bishain's lodge. He made a deliberate show of 'blessing' the resolution they had achieved.

Tangar quickly found Tarann and tried to explain what had happened. She listened patiently to his biased assessment of the matter but couldn't help notice that Talbot had spirited Barb away from the ceremony. She gestured at the pair that were quietly exploring possible connections they may have. "It seems that perhaps Bishain has found in your favor after all."

Molar grudgingly accepted Bishain's authority in the matter but met with Stanton and the enlightened-few for support. Their meeting involved a great deal of spirit-tea and ridicule of the old ways. From behind their wall of guardians, they boldly mocked the ceremonies and rituals of the elders, proclaiming freedom from the tyranny of "a dead god."

The meeting caught Thoma as he wandered across the commons. They tempted him with questions about the past and lured him into their tent. Stanton clasped him around the shoulders. "So old friend, how have you been? Sit with us and have some tea. We need someone that remembers the old chant – Branbush. Do you remember the words to the second verse?"

Thoma searched his mind as he casually found his talking wand in his pocket. It was a simple tune, that came easily, but why this august crowd of second level politicos would care about such an insignificant jingle puzzled him. He worried the wand with his thumb for a moment and quoted the verse easily. "Whisper of your heart and turn not to strife."

Stanton assessed his coherence. "Ha! That's it. I knew you could help. See, men, I told you we could use the wisdom of the old school. Come along old friend and join us. Have some tea. Tell us about what you've been doing."

As he ran his thumb repeatedly along the stick in his pocket, it developed a sliver at one of the junctures that concerned him. He had never noticed such an imperfection before. He started to withdraw the wand and then thought better of his actions. *This is not the place to show imperfections.* "Done alone."

"Ah, yeah, sure. Well, come back when you have a little more time. We'll keep a seat open for you." The bunch of intoxicated politicians snickered as the old man submissively bowed out.

Thoma made his way across the village commons and found himself once again outside the high-elder's door. Extracting his talking wand, he examined the flaw. As he ran his thumb along the contour, he couldn't detect the imperfection. He held it up to the light and carefully felt with his index finger.

"Thoma, it's good to see you again." Bishain stood in the doorway with a small group of courtiers.

The voice drew him away from his inspection. "It's gone."

Bishain dismissed the entourage with a wave of his hand. "What's gone?"

"A flaw." He gestured at the wand as the last of the reluctant supplicants grudgingly turned to leave.

"Come in and tell me about it. I often find that flaws vanish when I look closely. Maybe a sign of age…"

The two old friends soon sat by his hearth enjoying a cup of light tea with several temple attendants milling about. One girl seemed to be having a great deal of trouble arranging a bowel of fruit on a nearby table. Thoma watched the inept performance and feigned concern that the imperfection had vanished so completely. He held the wand out for scrutiny. "Sign on path."

Bishain's concern was with his friend, not the stick. "Yes, a sign... a sign has found you. When did you receive it?"

Thoma gestured across the commons and recollected with some satisfaction. "Few sing Branbush."

"Branbush? What do those fools care of Branbush?"

Thoma pointed to the knob where he had felt the imperfection. "Deception – of flawed path."

"Yes... Hail YodHeaVau. Thank You for this sign. What do you see in this flaw?"

Thoma glanced at the fruit girl, considered the wand for several moments, and then put it aside stirring his drink. "Tea clouds with time... Time clouds with tea."

Bishain smiled at the old truism. "As you see. You know, I talked with Tangar about the Blain girl. He seems to have a disagreement with Molar about just exactly what happened."

"Robes, not girl. Girl is without fault."

"Did you see the wound? Did Molar do the right thing?"

"Lust of enlightenment blindly sees no wrong."

"Speaking of lust... Why does he want to wed her?"

He glanced at the fruit girl and once again held his talking wand up for inspection running his thumb along its length. "Hidden flaw – hidden scar."

Nolan approached and whispered to Bishain.

"I'm sorry old friend, but I have to attend a meeting. The enlightened-few wish to speak of process. It seems, not everyone is happy with the pairings, and I'll bet I know who."

Thoma rose and headed for the side door. Stopping just at the threshold he looked cautiously at the fruit girl, stuffed his talking stick into his pocket, and spoke in undertones. "Hidden flaw."

A collection of low-level politicos that could best be described as a 'gang' awaited Bishain in the outer chamber. Each tribal bureaucrat wore a sash adorned with various feathers and trinkets that he assumed meant something to their imagined hierarchy. A guardian with a matching sash and carrying weapons accompanied each.

"All of you with weapons get out!" Bishain stood firm near the throne. When no one moved, he started for his inner chamber.

Stanton called to him. "Wait, we're here to talk with you."

Bishain glanced over his shoulder as he continued for the door. "Weapons are not allowed in this hall. Get out until you can be civil."

Stanton motioned to the band of guardians. "Comrades, please wait for us outside."

The grumbling caused Bishain to halt long enough to watch the disgruntled guards shuffle out. "Now, what is it that you wish to speak of?"

Molar stepped forward and began. "I want Tangar..."

"Stop! I've spoken with you already. I don't wish to listen to your complaints again. If no one else has anything to say, we are done here."

Stanton quickly stepped between the two men. "We've come to beg your understanding in the ways of the bonding. Molar here feels that his little disagreement with Tangar may have tainted his intent to wed, and wants to avail himself of your wisdom. He feels responsible for her and..."

"Silence! I've already heard this argument and my ruling stands. Now, unless there is something else… I have things to do."

"Master, please hear us out. Can you find some way that Molar may take his wife? It's not good for a man to go without a mate to balance his ways."

Bishain glanced scornfully at Molar. "The ceremony is over. Perhaps next year he will not be so eager to disrupt the ritual."

Stanton quickly blocked Molar's attempt to respond. "Perhaps you could extend the ceremony for another day. It would give those who didn't realize their desires to, perhaps, find someone. It would allow those who are less able to reconsider their position more – 'realistically' and select someone more suitable."

"You would diminish the worth of the bonding so that the unworthy can join. Don't you see how unfair that is to those who 'realized their desires', as you say"?

"It's more unfair to deny these people the opportunity to, at last, find someone befitting their shyness. They're just – timid. They only recognize their opportunity once it has passed. We, of the enlightenment, feel that these people deserve a second chance. Think of the children… The tribe needs the precious gift of children. These are not lesser people. They too deserve to bring new life and new ways to the people."

Bishain scanned the gang of enlightened followers. "Can you tell me that the children of these 'timid' ones will not also be timid? How are timid children good for the tribe? The only beneficiary I see of this proposed policy is Molar and he wasn't timid. He boldly accosted the Blain girl. And, now you ask that he be given a second chance to pursue this woman. No. I find nothing in your argument but hypocrisy, deceit, and treachery."

"You're, perhaps, too harsh in considering this deceit. The enlightenment enables us to recognize the needs of those less fortunate. We'll not be denied in bringing new ways to these poor people. Ways that fit their lives better than your outdated rituals of intolerance."

Bishain recognized that he would need to respond to the growing faction and turned to Molar. "If you truly wish to bond, bring a different woman. Bring a woman that will 'balance' your enlightened ways, not a child you have disfigured. I'll hold a second bonding for any that wish to participate. Nolan, make the announcement. Call for any who would like to partake in a bonding of the 'timid'."

Molar elbowed his way to the front. "Now wait a minute. I don't want to be stuck with some old looser that can't find anyone. I want Barb. I'm the only one that can take care of her. She'll need special treatment that only I can provide."

"Then your request isn't for the benefit of the 'less fortunate', as you claim, but for this one special case… Nolan, make the announcement. If you wish to participate, be there. If not, we'll be done with this bit of enlightenment."

The general population greeted Nolan's announcement with bewilderment and trepidation. No one had experienced such a departure from ceremonial norms. Most assumed that Beshain had buckled to the pressure of the enlightened-few since they openly celebrated the triumph and sophistication of their scheme.

People gathered to witness the ritual not knowing what to expect. Three couples from the enlightened-few joined the ceremony out of a perceived sense of duty to their cause rather than any evolution of their relationships. Molar stood by reveling in the impression of victory and searched the crowd looking for Barb.

Talbot stood as second assistant next to Nolan while he called the ritual to order. "Are there any others who wish to join at this time?"

The crowd mumbled and search for any that might seem undecided. Bishain stood behind his ministers and spoke softly to Talbot.

Talbot looked a bit surprised and searched his open hands for something he obviously didn't have as Bishain urged him to action. Scanning the crowd, he spotted Barb with a couple of her girlfriends. Moving cautiously through the crowd he stood in front of her with his hand extended and his head bowed. She looked bewildered and searched the crowd for her mother.

Mrs. Blain grabbed her husband by the arm and directed his attention. At first, he didn't understand what he was seeing but final grasped the situation. He whispered to his wife and nodded his approval.

Barb looked quickly to her girlfriends, as if they too needed to approve, then extended her hand to Talbot's grasp. He raised his head and smiled at her as he led their way back through the crowd to stand before Nolan.

Tangar cheered as he elbowed Stafon.

The commotion attracted the attention of Molar. Grudgingly assessing the situation, he grabbed at Maron standing nearby Lambert. She resisted only slightly as she quickly assessed Lambert's indifference, gulped the last of her wine, and tossed her cup to the ground. They formed up at the end of the small curving arc of couples standing in front of Nolan.

"Does anyone see any reason why these people should not wed?"

The crowd muttered but no one came forth.

Bishain stepped forward and, holding his arms open to the sky, turned with his scepter held high over Talbot and Barb. "Hail YodHeaVau. Bless these children of faith and hold them dear."

As he lowered the scepter, he passed it casually over the other couples. The gesture seemed to draw short of reaching Molar and his bride as the temple maidens began an impromptu rendition of the wedding song.

The ceremony broke up as Molar dragged his bride by the hand toward the wedding knoll. The three enlightened couples followed as the crowd dispersed, leaving the newlyweds to enjoy their bonding ritual. The soiled carpets and wilted flowers from the previous day still adorned the platform in a rather disappointing show of finery.

Talbot stood looking nervously at Barb. "I – I hope you don't mind. I mean, I hope you understand. I mean, I hope I can make you happy..."

Barb nervously watched the couples ascend the steps of the wedding platform. "I'm happy. I hope I can make you happy."

Tangar and Tarann approached the couple carrying wreaths of flowers and cups of wine. Sensing their unease with the expectation of having to join the pairing ritual, Tangar wrapped his arm around Talbot's shoulders. "Well, it's about time you showed some sense. Welcome to the club. Come on let's go see if we can find the others."

Tarann hugged Barb tightly for several moments as her parents joined them. Stafon and the others soon gathered and the party adjourned to her parent's tent.

The celebration wound down as evening crept into night. The village was still recovering from the previous night and found the enlightened ceremony clearly less festive. Molar and the enlightened couples continued their revelry well into the early hours while the rest of the world recovered quietly.

Talbot and Barb managed to steal away to complete their bonding in private and Tarann was able to hold Chilcoat to her heart's content. Tangar watched her motherly care with concern. He knew that she would come away from the evening filled with the joy of having held the precious bundle but saddened to the point of tears that the baby isn't hers.

As they got ready for their trip home, Tangar tried to be supportive but Tarann remained distant. "Don't worry; we'll have children – soon. It's in the scrolls." He tried to be lighthearted.

She looked coldly across the village commons. "No. We won't. We're never going to have a baby. The women are talking about us. They say I'm barren and should leave you to another. They say another woman should fulfill your needs."

"Those old biddies should mind their own business. We'll have a son for me and a daughter for you. It'll be just the way we wanted. I promise."

Her eyes brimmed with tears. "You can't promise such things. No one can. If God doesn't want me to have children, none of your promises mean anything."

"Maybe He doesn't want **me** to have children. Maybe it's my fault, not yours. Maybe you should find a new husband that can give you what you want."

She had already considered the idea but decided that it must be her fault. "It doesn't matter whose fault it is. I am wed to you, and unless you decide to put me out, I'll stay. If that means we'll never have children, so be it. I'll bear the shame of being your second wife. You can take another, younger, woman to give you the son you need."

"I don't want another wife. One is enough for any man. You're just upset because you held Catherin's baby. It does something to women. Get some rest. You'll feel better in the morning."

She pulled away from his attempt to reconcile. "This pain won't go away so easily. I'm a failure. I'm a dried up old hag just like the women say."

"You're not! Some day you'll have beautiful children to keep the knowledge of the way. It's in the scrolls..."

"Stop! I told you. I'll not have you curse me with such nonsense."

"It's not a curse. It's not nonsense. If I am to follow my father's ways, I must have faith that the scrolls are real. Don't you see? I'm to play a small part. Just as you are, just as our son and daughter are to play their parts. It's the only way that the 'one foretold' will come to save our people."

"Save our people from what? The only danger I see for our people is that they'll become fat and lazy."

"Save us from the enlightenment. Our daughter is be the 'Keeper of the way'; the one who will know the truth at the end of time."

"Why, why would you wish such a burden on our children? If that's the only way I'm to have children, I don't want them. I couldn't live knowing they're to suffer so."

"I'm sorry. Don't you see, their burden is our burden? The end will come, with or without our children. It's written. Hea will court Vau and start the cycle of life anew. His light will purge the world of the unworthy, just as He has done so many times before. It is to be a new beginning. If we accept our burden and prepare our children, they'll guide the people in the new world. If we fail, the enlightened-few will lead the people to ruin. YodHeaVau will begin the cycle without the children of the Shanare."

"I hate you and your stupid scrolls. I have no defense against such nonsense. It's not fair. You steal my children even before they're born." She turned and fled into their tent.

He remained at the evening fire smoking his pipe and wishing that he could make her understand that it wasn't his doings. He felt as helpless as she did, but he wanted to believe. He felt weak for wanting God to intervene and save him from living under the tyranny of the enlightenment. *I want to play a part in the downfall of Molar and his corruption but I have doubts myself. I doubt my understanding of the scrolls. I doubt the scrolls. I doubt God.*

He watched the smoke from his fire rush to meet the stars. The dogma he had learned from childhood told him that the spirits of the dead climb the tower of smoke to join the ancestors. He knew it was just a story told to children to ease the pain of losing a loved one, but it somehow comforted him. *Maybe she's right. Maybe the scrolls are nothing but fairytales and I'm being naïve to fall into such a trap. Hail YodHeaVau. If You do exist, give me a sign. Point the way. Show me how I am to serve.*

Chilbain struggled to secure his newly acquired baby furniture onto his cart. The various articulated cushions weren't heavy but they seemed to have a mind of their own that resisted being constrained. He grumbled to Tangar standing nearby watching the contest of wills. "I don't see the purpose of all this. The boy can sit up like the rest of us. He doesn't need to be coddled like some sort of prince."

"I'm sure Catherin would disagree with your assessment. He's her prince, and you better learn your place under him."

"Yeah, I'm sure. So, did you convince your old man to come home with you, or is he going to stay here?"

"I think he'll come home. Say, maybe I should take your cushions. They're a little small, but I might be able to get the old boy propped up with them. You know, sort of a throne for him to sit on. It sure would make the trip faster. I mean, stopping so he can catch up every few minutes really slows us down."

"Yeah, but he enjoys making you do it. It makes him feel like he's still in control. You wouldn't want to take that from him."

"I guess not. I mean, it's not like I have any choice."

Chilbain struggled pulling the cord tight around a plush pillow. "I know what you mean. So how's it working out with Barb? Is she going to fit in with Talbot?"

"Sure. Why not? He's a nice guy."

"Yeah, but she can be a handful. In case you haven't noticed."

"I've noticed. I think she's perfect for him. He's a little quiet. She can bring him out of his shell."

"Hmm, what about Molar? I thought you were going to get him deposed or something."

"Yeah, that didn't work out as well as I'd hoped. I mean, I think I got through to Bishain, but he still has to keep the enlightened-few appeased for now. They're a strong faction here and won't be denied. I think it's because of all the old people here. They just don't want to be bothered with all the political stuff so they let Stanton run everything."

"So what're you going to do about Molar then?"

"I don't know yet. I mean, I'd like to just put an arrow through him and be done with it, but that's just not the way of a Seer. I have to convince the people that he needs to be replaced. I was hoping that I could use Barb as a wedge to get people to listen."

"That doesn't sound very 'Seer' like either. I mean, how is your using a young girl better than what Molar had in mind?"

"Don't confuse me with ethics. You know what I mean. I just figured that people would see how Molar hurt her and would want to get rid of him."

"I think she's better off here. She doesn't need to be part of Molar's perversions or your quest for acceptance."

"I know. You're right. It just makes things harder for me."

"Don't your magic scrolls tell you what to do? Tarann said you've been spending a lot of time on them."

"Yeah, not really. I mean, I've spent a lot of time on them, but they don't make a whole lot of sense. Maybe I'm just too dense, but the way I understand them, we're in for some bad shit soon and nobody wants to hear that kind of stuff."

"Yeah Tarann said you cursed her with a witch-child."

"Tarann huh, what are you doing with my wife?"

"I was just babysitting. I guess you really pissed her off the other day. She came over and told Cat all about it. I was stuck in the other room trying to get Chilcoat to sleep."

"Yeah, she gets all worked up about babies, and I don't have much to tell her about it. I mean, I'm doing everything I know to do. So I told her about some of the stuff in one of the scrolls, and she got really pissed at me. I thought it might cheer her up to know that I saw those things."

"She said, you said, your daughter is going to be a witch. I mean, how did you think she was going to like that?"

"A good witch... Oh, you don't understand either. You'd have to read it."

"Not me – I have enough trouble just keeping junior happy. Speaking of which, I need to go see if I can find a goat for sale. Cat wants to put him on real food soon."

Tangar returned to his tent and considered his own packing duties. His cart remained largely naked at the side of his clearing. There were two tent panels and a couple of poles he hadn't used but, otherwise, it was not ready for the long trek back to the high mountain lake. The idea of a throne for his father lingered. *It's out of the question, of course, but still a tantalizing concept. He'd never allow himself to be carried like that; besides, I don't think I want to drag him up that pass anyway.*

He started gathering various utensils and tools scattered around their campsite.

Tarann peeked out at the commotion. "Are we leaving?"

"Yeah, might as well. Unless you have something else you want to do here."

"No. I'll be glad to get home. What about your dad, is he ready?"

"Of course not. You know him; he won't be ready until we're half way home. I'm going to try to keep up with Chilbain if you don't mind. The baby will slow them down a little, so maybe we can keep up."

"Why should I mind?"

"Well, you seem a little sensitive about the baby. That's all."

"Of course I'm sensitive, it's my nature. I want a baby and no amount of your blasphemy is going to change that, so get on with your life."

"That's the girl I married. Do you know where Dad is? I haven't seen him today."

"I chased him out just after breakfast. I think he headed for the elder's lodge."

"Oh great, I hope they haven't drugged him again. I'll be right back."

"How you fuss over him."

"It's my nature. You want a baby, well, I have one." He pulled his hat on and considered his spear for a moment but decided against it.

As he entered the elders lodge one of the guardians stopped him. "You're not welcome here. Only the elders of the awakening are allowed."

"Awakening my rump... I am the Seer of the lake tribe. Get out of my way."

Lambert joined his cohort. "You're not the Seer of anything, so get lost."

"Is my father here? I need to talk with him."

Lambert smirked knowingly to his friend as a great round of laughter came from the inner sanctum. "Your father's busy, can't you hear?"

Tangar clinched his fist around the spear he had opted not to bring. "I hear the sound of fools being foolish. I assume you're their butt." He moved cautiously toward the inner doorway, putting the first guard between himself and Lambert.

"I told you to get out of here!" Lambert grabbed around the guard at Tangar's arm.

Ducking quickly into the inner chamber, he scanned the room for his father. While Lambert's superior size gave him an advantage, Tangar's slender form and younger years allowed him to wriggle free and put several enlightened followers between them. Lambert grabbed him from behind and dragged him back. The scuffle soon brought the meeting to a halt as everyone turned to watch.

"Stop!" Stanton called from a platform at the far end of the room. "Just what do you think you're doing?"

Lambert caught Tangar and wrestled him to a stop. "Sorry Master. He wormed past me."

Stanton smirked at the display. "Release him. There's no need for conflict. What's so urgent that you must interrupt our meeting?"

Tangar spotted the unruly tuft of his father's hair across the room as he pulled his arm free. "Dad, come with me. We're getting ready to leave."

"Oh, now, wait a minute. He was just telling us a story. You wouldn't want to interrupt before he gets to the moral would you?"

"The moral is always the same. 'Good triumphs over evil'. Come on Pop; let's let these children 'study' on their own."

Thoma calmly pointed to a spot on his talking stick. "Song of way away."

Tangar assessed the blemish and smirked. It was, indeed, the marks associated with the story of children singing and climbing the ladders to heaven. He knew that his father reserved the story for belligerent children that had gone astray. "Well chosen. Come on. Let's see if we can get you set up for the trip."

Stanton watched the dealings with confused annoyance. "Now wait a minute. Thoma, old friend, you've spoken of staying on here in our little village. You could be a real help here. Think of the children. Your knowledge of the old ways can be of use in teaching the young right from wrong. That sounds like a good idea, doesn't it? You can be in charge of explaining the 'wisdom' of the old ways."

Tangar knew that his father's interpretation of the scrolls would serve only for ridicule. "That's OK. We need him at home. Right Pop? You want to be there when Tarann has your grandkids, right?"

Molar coughed spitefully. "The only way Tarann is going to have any kids is for a real man to take over for you."

The crowd laughed knowingly and turned to Tangar. "Molar, I think the time has come for you to return to your own village and leave me and my people alone."

He grabbed Maron and pulled her reluctantly under his arm. "Well, it doesn't matter, what you think. Your village is my village now. My wife is of the lakeshore clan and that makes me a member of the tribe. You don't need to concern yourself with being the Seer anymore."

"No. You're wrong... I am the rightful holder of the Seer's robes. You're an outsider, you can't be our Seer."

"That's where **you're** wrong. I've been your Seer since your old man – slipped away, and I'm going to remain your Seer until you can convince the high council otherwise. And, I just don't see that happening any time soon. Your failure to awaken unto the light means none of the 'few' will support your bid. And, without that, you're never going to rise to be Seer."

"I've seen the light you speak of, and it's nothing more than false readings of the scrolls. You pick only vague snippets and distort them into lies to cover your corrupt dealings. You separate people from their God with false claims of wisdom and hide behind a wall of guards drinking tea that you say gives you insight into the hearts of men. Well, it doesn't. Those herbs give insight only into the heart of the Seer that uses them wisely. They aren't meant as a party favor."

He swept his hand across the nearby table and dumped a large beaker of tea onto the floor. "To use them as you do leads only to distortions of truth that trick you into believing your foolishness is wisdom. These are lessons from the sacred scrolls of the old ways. You should heed this warning, for the scrolls tell of hard times to come. They tell of a man that will lead the people, and a golden child yet to be born that will know the true meaning of all that is written."

"You make too much of nonsensical poems and songs in those old rags. The awakening has shown us the truth. It's not found in the flowery gibberish of doom saying, but in the simple knowledge of birth and death, of marriage and commitment, that we have built our lives upon. We are a stronger people without the dependence on such an unfeeling god. We've put Him in His place. We use the herbs to strengthen our union among men, not some mystical message of wisdom. We know what these herbs are and we use them as we see fit. You see, that is where the old ways are wrong. We are the masters, not just pawns in some game of spirits and charms. That's why I'm the Seer, and you are simply a pretender clinging to a pile of old rags waiting for a dead god to save you."

Tangar grabbed Thoma by the hand and led him away.

As the years passed, Chilcoat grew into a strong young lad while Thoma seemed to grow feebler with every passing month. The tribe went to the gathering each winter and the friction between Tangar and Molar simmered just below the boiling point with occasional minor acts of rebellion and meaningless reprimands. The new way continued to seek favor; however, Bishain managed to retain leadership and continued to support their secretive study of the ancient scrolls.

Tangar's friendship with Talbot and Stafon evolved from buddies to colleagues with the common goal of continuing the old ways. Stafon rose to assume the role of Seer of the Western Clan when his mentor died in a diving accident.

Their annual effort of studying the sacred scrolls grew more precious and critical to their development as Seers in the old traditions. The birth and death scrolls remained as the only links to the past for the enlightened-few. They were thoughtfully preserved and transcribed; however, the remaining four scrolls suffered the ruthless savagery of neglect.

While the fragile parchments were the core of their study efforts, they dared not copy them. The instructions contained within their text demand a strict process of transcription oversight that the trio couldn't provide. This was of particular concern for the sixth scroll. They repeatedly took up the challenge of trying to decipher the text. It was near gibberish with many flowery passages and poetic diversions that confused all attempts at meaningful understanding. From what they could tell, that particular scroll is to be known only to the One foretold when he presents it to the Keeper.

Talbot approached Bishain when returning the packet of scrolls. "Master, we're still unable to grasp some of what's said in the sixth scroll. Is there someone that can help us understand?"

"What do you know of that text?"

"Well, to be honest, not very much. It seems that we are to keep it for 'The One'. Other than that, it's all too vague and full of fantasies."

"Then you understand what you need to know. Each of us is destined to serve a specific task. You and your friends are to keep the old ways so that The One will understand."

Tangar stood by impatiently. "That's it? We spent all this time studying those things, and all we needed to know is that we're just to keep them safe so someone else can figure them out?"

Bishain turned to him thoughtfully. "I believe, with time, you will find wisdom in what you've done. Pray in the old way. It will bring understanding."

***

Thoma, once again, insisted that he could walk up a particularly treacherous section of the trail returning over the mountain pass. Tangar pulled his cart off the trail as best he could to wait for him to catch up. An early spring storm soaked the narrow path carved into the cliff face and made the normally difficult trek almost impossible for the old man.

Tangar returned along the trail to 'encourage' his father. *He won't accept a hand but he'll allow inspirational taunts.*

Chilbain noted their delay, pulled alongside, and set to work rebalancing the load on his cart. The women huddled together against the incessant wind and had a light snack while he unloaded some tent panels with Chilcoat's 'assistance'. He used three poles extending into the path to form a ramp stretching up the back of the platform. As he struggled to shove the awkward bundles up the ramp and back into place, Chilcoat asked questions about his goal, his methods, and his shoes.

Molar and Lambert soon appeared coming up the trail. Their oversized carts burgeoned with trinkets and keepsakes from the gathering. As they approached, it became obvious that they couldn't pass until Chilbain finished his task.

Lambert parked his cart unnecessarily close. "Get this crap out of the way. The Seer needs to pass."

Chilbain paused and leaned against the bundle halfway up the ramp. Wiping the sweat from his brow, he considered his challenger. "Chilc, why don't you go get me a drink from Mom while these gentlemen lend me a hand?"

Lambert scoffed and looked to Molar for direction. He took a slight nod as a cue and kicked a pole from the ramp structure. The tent bundle tipped precariously for a moment then scattered the remaining poles and fell to the ground in a soggy lump.

Chilbain grabbed at the load trying to prevent the cart from tipping then scrambled for a weapon. The best he could find was a tent pole. It didn't work very well as a spear, but he managed to cram it though the wheels of Lambert's cart. The scuffle that ensued lasted for only a few moments, for while Lambert was a formidable hunter, his recent predilection for wine didn't serve him well against Chilbain's robust stature.

Tangar and Thoma soon arrived to witness Chilbain standing triumphant over Lambert. Tangar drew his bow to action while Molar remained cautiously hidden behind his new wife.

Lambert's gasping form quickly assessed his failed quest and decided to check his cart for damage. Extracting the pole, he stood considering its use as a bludgeon but decided, instead, to toss it off the cliff.

Maron stood by snickering and covered her face to hide her delight with the act of bravado.

Chilbain watched with considerable irritation. *The pole is easily replaced, but the insult isn't so easily ignored.* He walked calmly to Lambert's cart, pulled a full wine skin from the load, and tossed it off the cliff. "Your turn."

Two more carts were now approaching from the downhill trail. Lambert clinched his jaw and contemplated his next move. "This isn't over."

Chilbain returned to his cart. "I'd be disappointed if you said it was."

Lambert and Molar quickly gathered their things and moved awkwardly around the cart. The two other families followed in quick succession leaving Tangar and Chilbain to wrestle the tent bundle back onto the platform.

The remaining journey back to the high lake meadow was uneventful and largely silent for Tangar. Tarann questioned him at the evening fire. "You're bothered by something. Do you want to talk?"

"The scuffle with Lambert bothers me. I mean, Chilbain's a spirited character but, he wasn't the cause of the conflict. Lambert was just following Molar's orders. That assault was meant for me. He's such a coward that he uses a dupe like Lambert to attack my friends rather than face me."

"Why would he do that? You're no threat to him."

"He fears my knowledge of the old ways. I think, perhaps, Nolan has betrayed us. Molar knows that we are keeping the knowledge and that threatens him. He knows that if the people ever realize how corrupt and weak the new ways are, they'll turn on him and he can't allow that. He'll do anything, or rather, he'll promise them anything to keep them ignorant."

"So what are you going to do?"

He sat silent for several moments contemplating various plans of attack. "I'm going to pray. That's what Bishain said to do. It doesn't seem like enough..."

"God will help. It'll be enough."

Tangar looked at the woman he loved in a new light. *She's afraid. She's afraid that I'm going to do something foolish, something that will take me from her. I can't allow her to be afraid of a fool like Molar.*

He cleared the carpet from floor by the fire and etched prayer circles into the clay. Placing various trinkets into the figure to represent those of concern from the conflict, he chanted perplexing verses from the scrolls.

Tarann watched thoughtfully trying to understand his torment. She had seen Thoma perform the same ritual many times, but had always assumed it was just his feeble mind. To now see her husband perform such a ceremony worried her in ways she couldn't put into words. She felt she was losing him to something she didn't understand. "Should you be doing this? Isn't it forbidden?"

"**Forbidden** is a little harsh. Let's just say it is discouraged by the enlightened-few, but that means less and less to me all of the time. They have no right to deny me God."

"Am I to keep this secret then?"

"**Secret** is also perhaps a little harsh. Let's just keep it between us for now. It is something between a husband and his wife that needn't concern others."

"And God."

"Hmm, yes, and God."

The weeks of spring soon faded into the warmth of summer and the first harvest of fruit was on the vines. Everyone was in a festive mood. Several young families ventured to the upper meadow to gather berries and enjoy the morning sun. Chilbain and Catherin found a large bush trailing up a sharp embankment bordering the meadow. They settled in, gathering hands full of the delicate fruit while Chilcoat played nearby laughing and chasing bees.

Lambert suddenly appeared. "Ah, I'm glad you've seen fit to harvest the Seer's fruit for him."

Chilbain turned to address him. "This fruit belongs to the finder. These vines grow at the whim of Vau and no one owns their bounty but Her."

"That's where you're wrong. The master claims his due, and you are selected to provide an offering of the first fruits." He bent to retrieve a nearly full basket.

Chilbain grabbed him by the hair and pulled him away. "Tell your 'master', if he thinks he's man enough to claim my labor he should do it himself instead of sending his lackey."

Chilcoat began to cry, attracting the attention of several of the other families scattered across the meadow. Catherin comforted him as Lambert straightened his hair and tried to appear unruffled. "This isn't over."

"You said that already."

Lambert left with only the slightest glance back at the sympathetic crowd and the vines winding up the cliff face.

The party spirit resumed with a couple of the neighbors stopping by to ask about the altercation. By early afternoon, the family relaxed in the shade of the cliff. Chilbain lay with his head on Catherin's lap as she struggled to wash Chilcoat's face. He showed the telltale sign of eating too many berries and his eyes drooped from his busy day.

Suddenly a rock fell next to her. She looked up in horror as she recognized the cliff beginning to collapse on them. She flung Chilcoat away as hard as she could and screamed. "Run!"

Tangar stood in shock at the scene. He had been in the highlands tending the roses for Molar. His mind wouldn't accept that his lifelong friends were dead.

No one had any knowledge of what had happened. The only thing anyone knew for sure was that a rockslide killed them. Tangar grabbed one of the workers clearing the rubble. "Where's the boy? Where is Chilcoat?"

"I don't know. He was here a while ago. Somebody must've taken him to Molar. His leg was broken."

Lambert intercepted Tangar as he burst through the door of Molar's hut. "He's busy. Go away."

"Get out of my way!" Tangar attempted to push past him.

Lambert stood his ground and struggled with him. "I said he's busy. Now, get out of here!"

Tangar searched for something he could use to beat Lambert into submission but found nothing. "Look, I need to talk to him. I want to see the boy."

"I told you, he's busy. Now, get out of here before I... Just leave. Now!"

He could hear Chilcoat crying. Molar was apparently trying to quiet him, but wasn't having much luck. Tangar struggled between anguish and panic. *I have to get the boy away from Molar before he decides to butcher him too. God, have You no mercy? For the boy's sake, will You please guide my hand against him?*

The admonishment of his years of training came to him and he uttered the only prayer he knew God would listen to. "Hail YodHeaVau. Whisper ever gently on his soul."

Quickly returning to his hut, he grabbed his spear. As he turned to leave, the butt of the weapon clipped the cooking shelf and knocked a pot into the fire. A shower of sparks rose through the smoke vent as the tea hissed and nearly put the flame out. Smoke and steam filled the hut with a chocking haze that burned his eyes.

He used the spear to prod the pot out of the embers and again turned to leave. Gazing tearfully at his spear, he considered his skill with the weapon. *Lambert is likely to turn this on me before I'm able to get to the boy. I don't want to get killed, but I have to get the boy.*

The fire was beginning to take hold again as the flames dried the wood. A small branch flared to life and cleared the air as its heat rose quickly through the smoke vent. He grabbed the branch and held it in the flame for a moment. "Yod, please find wisdom in what I do."

Moving quickly around the back of Molar's hut, he placed the burning branch against the side of the structure. It dimmed for a moment and started to discolor the fabric. Hefting his spear uncertainly, he moved to the front of the tent, rattled his lance against the doorpost, and shouted. "Molar, I've come to see the boy."

Lambert stuck his head out for a moment and then quickly returned with his spear held at the ready. "I've told you for the last time to leave. If you're going to insist, I'll put an end to this right now."

Tangar moved away cautiously. Glancing quickly over the roof of the hut, he noticed smoke beginning to trail up from the far side. "Look Lambert, I don't have an issue with you. I just want to talk with Molar about helping the boy — Chilcoat. It's my job."

"I don't care what you want. I'm telling you..."

Molar suddenly burst out of the tent nearly knocking the spear from Lambert's hands. "Fire! Fire! Don't just stand there, get some water!"

His ceremonial robes flared open revealing his naked form as he ran across the clearing clutching a jar of muddy brown tea. Maron followed, chocking and coughing, as she awkwardly carried his medicine bag and several prized possessions to safety.

Lambert stood confused for several moments but eventually dropped his lance and ran toward the lake. Molar glared at Tangar for a moment before following Lambert to the lake.

Quickly ducking into the tent, Tangar dragged Chilcoat over his shoulder and staggered out of the smoke filled room. As he emerged from the choking cloud, he caught a glimpse of Chilbain and Catherin standing stoically across the clearing dressed in their finest ceremonial garb.

By now, several of the neighbors had joined the bucket brigade and watched in disbelief as the pair emerged coughing and chocking from the structure. The man at the front of the line grabbed the next bucket offered to him and emptied it over the smoldering duo.

By the time their shower ended, the vision of Chilbain and Catherin had disappeared... Tangar shook his head several times to clear his thoughts and stole away with Chilcoat in the confusion as Molar stood by shouting orders.

Tarann held the boy close, cradling him tightly, while Tangar pulled his leg straight and braced it in a tight wrap.

The trauma was beginning to wear off leaving Chilcoat in a great deal of pain. "Mommy! ... I want my mom! It hurts. It hurts really bad. I want my mom!"

Tarann began to cry as she rocked him. She had never realized how little she knew about being a mother. "I know babe. I know. It'll be better in a little while. You'll see. It'll be better soon. Just be brave a little longer."

Tangar knew of several herbs that would take the ache from his knee, but nothing that would take the grief from his heart. The thought of Molar stealing away with his jug of tea crossed his mind. *No! The pain of reality is better than that escape into dependence.*

When, at last, Chilcoat nodded off. Tangar rose to store away his cache of herbs. "I have to go face Molar. He'll want the boy back."

Tarann caressed him gently. "He can't have him! He's mine now. He's mine!"

The townsfolk quickly brought the conflagration under control and everyone stood around asking the same unanswered question. "What happened?"

Tangar approached the group with his spear held at the ready. "I have Chilcoat. He's safe for now and sleeping comfortably."

Molar looked disheveled in his soot-smudged finery. "I know what you've done. Don't think that you're fooling anyone."

One of the bystanders offered. "I saw him. He saved the boy. He carried him to safety."

Molar seethed at the insolence. "The boy be damned. He saved him from the fire he set. Is that the hero you would have him?"

Tangar sensed support from some of the crowd. "I noticed that your hands were full saving your tea and I wanted to know if the boy needed help. If I am to be blamed for something, let it be that."

"You want to save him? Bring him to me. He needs my attention. The tea I saved is medicine for him. That's why I have it. He needs this medicine soon or he'll lose his leg."

"He doesn't need your drugs. I've already treated him and he'll be fine now that he's with his family."

Lambert interrupted with a bit more satisfaction than was fitting. "His family is gone. He's a burden on the tribe now and he'll never walk again. He should've died with his father."

Several of the enlightened supporters grumble agreement.

A flush of realization swept through Tangar as he remembered his vision of Chilbain and Catherin. "Chilcoat is my son now. He'll not be a burden on anyone. It's written... He'll grow strong and brave, and lead the tribe through times of great suffering."

Molar drained the pot he held in one quick gulp. "According to the high-elder, you're still my apprentice. I'll not have such threats of revolt preached by you or anyone else."

"I speak only of what's written in the sacred scrolls of the Shanare."

"Your fascination with those forgotten scraps of the past doesn't serve you well. You'd be wise to forget that nonsense and awaken unto the light of the new way. That boy is a ward of the tribe now and he'll need to earn his keep serving those above him. If he's unable because you've not allowed me to treat him properly, you'll need to contribute your earnings to make up the difference."

"I'll gladly contribute whatever you wish to keep you from butchering him the way you did Barb."

"You can start by contributing the three tent panels you've ruined."

"I don't have three tent panels."

"Well, you'd better find them. The Seer of the lake clan cannot be without fitting shelter. I'll be waiting." Molar grabbed his scepter from Maron, standing by submissively, and waved it over Tangar as if making an official proclamation.

The funeral pyre for Catherin and Chilbain drew the entire village in somber reflection.

Chilcoat insisted that he should attend despite Tarann's misgivings. Tangar fortified the boy with an extra dose of pain medication and supported him as they hobbled across the clearing.

Molar appeared in his dirty robes, obviously drunk from his spirit-tea, and stumbled his way through the ceremony. He mumbled something incoherent about Chilbain finally awakening unto the light and read from a bastardized copy of the death scroll. "The smoke of Yod's forgiveness carries these humble spirits to drift among the clouds and forever live above the sky."

Chilcoat remained stoic through the debacle despite, or perhaps because of, his pain.

Molar eventually staggered away with his entourage of the enlightened-few and allowed true friends to approached Chilcoat with gifts of remembrance and assurance that "things will get better."

Tears streaked Chilcoat's face as he watched the last embers of the fire flicker. Tangar solemnly performed a memorial chant and approached the boy with Chilbain's weapons held in offering. "The weapons of your father are yours now. Do with them as you see fit."

The spear and bow were magnificent works of deadly art with serpents and lions painted on their robust frames. The rockslide left two arrows broken and the spear had a distinct gouge just below the handgrip.

Chilcoat pulled the broken arrows from the quiver and gazed tearfully at their ruined form.

Sensing the boys torment, Tangar pulled an arrow from his own quiver, snapped it in half, and placed it on the flame. "Sleep well old friends and know that your son has found a loving home."

Chilcoat's face twisted in anguish as he watched the flames eagerly consume the offering. He looked pleadingly to Tangar as his fist clinched the broken shafts. He held them sheltered in his grasp until he realized he had drawn blood on the jagged edges. Slowly opening his grip, he carefully straitening the bloodstained shafts and placed them side-by-side on the dwindling flames.

The flames flared to greedily consume the offering and then died to mere embers. Tangar couldn't help but question his faith. *If there really is a god of all things, why would he be so cruel to the young? First Barb, and now Chilcoat… What possible purpose could it serve to hurt the innocent while scum like Molar go unpunished?*

Pulling himself from his reflection he resolved, for the benefit of those gathered, to show the faith he didn't really feel. He repeated the last verse of the memorial chant, combed his hand through the warm ashes and then pressed them to his chest. "Two spirits are now one. I'll miss you both dearly."

Chilcoat watched this final act of remembrance, bravely grabbed a handful of ashes, but then simply stared at them in his half-opened palm.

Tangar started to reach for his hand to help but recognized it is nothing that can be helped or forced. A tear escaped and blurred his vision as he caught a glimpse of Chilbain warmly holding the boy's hand…

***

By midmorning, Tangar set about trying to find tent panels to replace those damaged by the fire. In his estimation, he really only needed two since the third panel was only discolored. Rather than argue the point with Molar, he elected to use it himself and pulled one of the panels from his own hut in its place.

He noted the scorch mark made a distinctive wing-like arc across the panel. It bore an uncanny resemblance to the wing of a nighthawk. The stealthy little creature plied the night skies of the highland lake and was the symbol of the lakeshore tribe. To have it now stunningly appear as the result of his desperate act seemed somehow to make and appropriately bold statement about his acceptance of responsibility for the fire. He took a charred branch from the pyre and added a few details to the wing panel that he then used at the front of his hut for all to see.

Through mild coercion of his friends, he negotiated a second panel. The third panel proved the hardest to find since everyone feared Molar's reprisal. He final resolved to dismantle Chilbain's tent and traded one of the panels for a tattered one from a neighbor.

The solemn task of disassembling the structure progressed slowly. The clothing and personal items feel to Tarann for disposition while Tangar tried to determine if he could save or use any of the household items. He used much of the remaining structure to add a room to his own hut to accommodate Chilcoat. It lent a comforting air of familiarity and permanence to his new home.

Tarann nursed the boy as best she knew how. His youth responded well physically and he was soon up walking but he remained sullen and emotionally unresponsive. No one could blame him, but it grated hard on her motherly instincts.

As the seasons passed, she tried everything she could think of to turn the boy into the child she had longed for.

He sensed her frustration but resisted her advances. *I like her. I can even say that I've grown to love her, but she isn't my mom. I just wish she'd stop trying to be her.*

Thoma sat by the hearth in the elder's hut tracing his prayer circles on the floor. Caran, the attending maiden, brought him a cup of tea. "I wish you'd stop doing that. You're making a mess."

She and her younger sister, Charona, were Stafon's wards from the western village. Tangar had seen to it that they found comfort in serving the elders. The pair was nearly inseparable and doted over Thoma in shifts that allowed him to displace the girl that spied on him.

He enjoyed antagonizing Caran in particular. She had a motherly aura that contrasted sharply with her cherub like features. For, while Charona was the younger sister, she looked more mature, much to the irritation of her sister and the delight of the young men of the tribe.

Thoma sensed Caran's frustration and tried to make up for it by showing preference for her attention. This usually took the form of what he considered 'good natured' teasing. He reflected on her words for a moment and brushed the dust he had created toward her. "Help."

"That's all you have to say? 'Help' – I'll help alright. I'll get you a broom so you can sweep all this up."

He thoughtfully trailed his hand over a collection of trinkets gathered nearby and selected a smooth, attractively marbled, stone. Holding it up toward her, he squinted as if measuring its fit and placed it on the left side of the diagram.

She pursed her lips and turned to leave. "Finish your tea. I don't have time for your nonsense."

Tangar approached with a small package of fruit. "Hey Pop, how are you? I see you're up to no good."

Chilcoat followed reluctantly shuffling across the room watching Caran leave.

"Help."

"Yes, I suppose it does. You remember Chilcoat don't you?" He gestured at the boy still bashfully watching Caran.

"Foretold."

Chilcoat broke his gaze to acknowledge the old man. They were actually old friends but, each time they met, they had to go through an introduction as if they were strangers just to be sure the old man remembered him. "Hey Gramps, how have you been?"

Thoma gazed thoughtfully at the pair, selected two icons from his collection, and placed them within the prayer circles. He winked at Chilcoat and moved his icon next to the stone he had placed for Caran. "Speak boldly."

Tangar smirked at the old man's humor. "We're headed up to the falls. I don't suppose you want to come along."

"Not of Spirit."

"No... Bird hunting. The boy's going to teach me how to use a bow." Tangar ruffled Chilcoat's hair.

He dodged away from further assault and straightened the bow slung over his shoulder. "Not if we don't get going."

He had crafted the bow two years earlier at Tangar's knee. For while he was large and very strong for his age, his father's bow was still too stout for him to draw. It remained propped against the wall of his room in a commemorative shrine he had fashioned. He carried one of his dad's arrows in his quiver, but he never used it. It too was a sacred token that accompanied him as a warm reminder of the past. He wanted to remember his folks, but as he grew older, he found it harder to get a clear picture of them. The rock fall still burned in his memory, but only as a cruel whim of the gods. No details of the day remained, only a vague distrust for anything attributed to God.

Thoma considered the assemblage of trinkets on the diagram and nudged his own token deep into the arms of Vau. "Spirit walks with guide of knowledge."

Tangar winced at his father's apparent loss of focus and headed out the door. "Yes. I'm sure He does."

The trek to the falls was nothing more than a diversion. Tarann had been particularly moody and insisted that the 'boys', as she called them, get out of her house. She had cleaning to do and didn't want them around.

Chilcoat also seemed moody. He normally didn't talk much, but he was particularly quiet as the pair negotiated the steep trail leading up to the falls. After a quick rest for his knee, he dispatched a plump young quail while Tangar built a small fire.

Tangar finally broke the silence. "Is there something bothering you?"

"Nah, I've just been thinking. That's all."

"About what? I mean, anything I can help with?"

"Nah. I was just wondering about Gramps. He doesn't seem to be doing very well. I mean, he's healthy enough, I guess, but he just doesn't make much sense anymore. You know what I mean?"

"Yeah, he has his ups and downs. Mostly down lately... I think maybe your girlfriend is slipping him some herbs in his tea to keep him quiet."

"She's not my girlfriend!"

"I saw the way you looked at her. You're not fooling anyone."

"Don't change the subject. I'm worried about him."

"Yeah, me too... I'm afraid we're going to have to let him stay at the gathering village this year. I've been putting it off, but he'll probably be better off there. They'll know how to care for him."

"You don't think they'll put herbs in his tea?"

"Yeah, probably, but maybe that'll be a good thing. He'll be happy."

"Aren't you just putting him away then?"

He hesitated to answer. The reality of the question stung. "Yeah, maybe. There comes a time... Maybe you'll do the same for me someday."

"Is that what you want?"

"Yeah, maybe. Maybe it'll hurt less."

"You know it won't."

"I'd like to think that it would. I don't want to ever hurt you."

Tarann prepared the bird and the family sat quietly considering the day's events. The boys were respectful of her mood as she somberly worked her task. The solemn mood drove Chilcoat to quickly finish the meal and retire to his room.

Tarann sat silently at the hearth while Tangar lit his pipe. She finally whispered almost imperceptibly. "I think I'm pregnant."

"What? You're what?"

"I think maybe I'm going to have a baby."

He dropped his pipe and grabbed her warmly. "That's great! Isn't it?"

"I – I don't know. I mean, of course it's great, if – if the baby's healthy."

"Of course, why wouldn't he be healthy?"

"The women say I'm too old. They say my baby will be a burden on them, on the tribe."

"Don't listen to them. They don't know what they're talking about. He'll be fine. You'll be fine. Everything will be great."

"I don't feel great. I'm scared."

"Of course you're scared. I'm scared too. I mean, everyone gets scared when they're pregnant. It's a scary thing. I mean, bringing a whole new person into the world is scary."

"It's not just that. I mean, I don't feel good. Everyone says they feel wonderful when they're pregnant. I don't feel wonderful. I feel like something's wrong. Like the baby's sick or something. I dread waking up. Every morning something else seems to be wrong with me."

"Lots of women get sick at first. You'll be OK. I'll make you some tea. It'll make you feel better."

"I don't want your witches brew. I just want my baby to be healthy."

Tangar was beside himself trying to contain his excitement. *Tarann told me, "don't jinx it by telling everyone," but I have to tell someone. These are the times I miss Chilbain the most. Chilcoat will have to do. He deserves to know.*

"... and, so, Mom's going to have a baby."

Chilcoat remained somber. "Does that mean I have to move out?"

"What? No. Don't be silly. It just means you're going to have a baby brother, or sister. It'll be great. You can teach him to hunt, and fish, and all sorts of things. It'll be fun. You'll see."

"Where's it going to sleep?"

"We'll figure out something, don't worry. In the meantime, don't tell anyone. Mom wants to keep it secret for a while."

"What about Gramps? He needs to know."

"Hmm. Yes, maybe I'll tell him at dinner tonight. First, I need put some meat on the table; maybe a hog, or an elk, something to celebrate."

"You'll need some help then."

"Of course I'll need your help. You must always have a second when hunting. That's why I'm here. You're my faithful man foretold."

As the pair made their way along the western trail, Chilcoat tried his best to seem mature. "What is all that crap Gramps keeps saying; 'Keeper of man foretold'? It's creepy."

"It's the way of the Seer, as written in the sacred scrolls. You want me to teach you?"

"No thanks. Not if it does that to me. I mean, how come he's not the Seer anymore? If he knows all that stuff, how come we're stuck with Molar? He doesn't talk like that."

"No. Molar follows the new ways of enlightenment. He has little use for God or His scrolls. He uses them only to bully people with rules contrived from verses they twist to serve their purpose. Papa is of the old school. He finds things in the scrolls that few others see. For that, and his unwillingness to bend to their ways, someone poisoned him. At least, that's what I think happened. He did a reading at the gathering a few years back that revealed the corruption of the new ways and foretold of frightening times to come. They pretended to applaud his effort and gave him tea to celebrate his findings. He's never been the same since. They pulled Molar in until a new Seer can be trained and said his findings are to remain secret until they verify what he said."

"Then they're looking into it?"

"Not really, that's just what they tell anyone that asks: 'They're forming a study group and will report on their findings'. The scrolls are some pretty vague stuff. It's hard to say exactly what they mean. I mean, some of that stuff is obviously fantasy. I mean, people living under water, floating in the air, and living above the sky. That's just crazy. The enlightened-few claim these things are simply fables for the ignorant that should be forgotten, and it's hard to argue with their logic."

"You've read them. What do they mean to you?"

"They mean I'm too ignorant to understand… Enough of this jabbering, we're scaring the game away. You go get set down in that gully and I'll scare something your way."

The meal turned out to be a small peccary that Tarann prepared but didn't eat. Thoma came and brought Caran along as his attending nurse. He thought it would be funny to aggravate Chilcoat with her presence. Neither she nor Chilcoat seemed to appreciate this bit of levity. They both sat silently throughout the meal, only acknowledging the other when forced to. None the less, Thoma seemed to get a great deal of satisfaction out of making the pair participate in minor social exchanges such as passing awkward plates and bowls when not really needed.

As the meal finished, Caran helped clear the dishes and Tangar lit his pipe. Passing it to Thoma he finally spoke. "So Pop, I have some news for you, but I want you to keep it secret." He looked cautiously to Tarann and discretely tried to be sure Caran didn't hear. "We're going to have a baby."

Thoma leaned in to hear and his face contorted as if in pain. "I'm sorry for this grief my children, but the time isn't right."

Tangar was near rage. "What do you mean, 'not right'? Of course it's right you old fool. It's up to Vau not you."

By now, Tarann recognized what had happened. "What's going on?"

Tangar grabbed his pipe as Thoma attempted to pass it to Chilcoat. "Nothing, I was just telling Pop our news. He doesn't seem to appreciate it."

Thoma looked to her. "Patients child, the Keeper will come."

She looked horrified. "Don't you dare curse my child with your witches' scrolls and potions. I'll not have it!"

He held his hand out for Caran to help him stand. "Rejoice for Vau embraces your warmth."

Chilcoat sensed the awkwardness of the room and grabbed the old man by the arm. "Come on Gramps, I'll help you home."

Thoma seemed almost to caress the hand on his arm. "Yes, wisdom of the man..." Waving weakly to Caran he shuffled toward the door. "Come along child, we've overstayed our welcome."

Caran gave a timid nod of thanks to Tarann, pursed her lips in determination, and followed the pair out the door.

Tarann was near tears as she finished cleaning up. "Your father is so – frustrating. Doesn't he realize what he's saying? What's he thinking? Does he think I'm supposed to be happy that he curses me with those damn scrolls? Does he think at all?"

"That's a good question. I'm not sure that anything he says has anything to do with thinking. You can't let him bother you. He's – sick. I don't know what else to call it."

"I know what to call it... He's mean. He thinks he can wander around drinking spirit-tea and saying anything that pops into his head and people are supposed to think he's crazy or sick. Well, I don't buy it. I think he knows what he's saying. I think he's hiding behind his 'illness'. He's just hiding from Stanton and the enlightenment."

Tangar had frequently considered such things. "It would explain a lot, but I just don't want to believe he's that – weak. He's always been there for me. Maybe there's something in what he says. I mean, he is a Seer. You, yourself, said you don't feel good. Maybe he sees that. Maybe he sees that the baby is sick..."

"No! Don't even think such things. Get out! Get out of my sight. I don't want to even see your face if you're going to say such things."

***

Tangar sat silently at the dawn watch. It would be hours until sunrise, but the solitude fit his mood. The sky swam with countless stars in the clear mountain air and gave him perspective on his insignificance. *I have to make Tarann understand. He's my dad. I can't just tell him that I think he's full of crap. He thinks he's helping with wisdom from the scrolls. Maybe that's the key. Maybe if he shows me what he's talking about I'll understand better and then I can explain it to her. The only problem with that is the scrolls are at the gathering village and it's still months until the gathering. By then she'll have forgotten all about it and the baby will nearly be here.*

It suddenly occurred to him that the trek back from the gather would be a difficult undertaking with both his father and a very pregnant wife or newborn in tow. *Maybe I'll leave him there this year. That would solve everything. It may not do him any good, but she wouldn't have to listen to his ramblings anymore and the journey home would be much easier.*

Lambert approached with his spear at the ready. "Ah, there you are. What's the matter, the wife kick you out?"

Tangar snapped back from his wanderings. "Yeah, something like that."

"Molar wants you to do something."

"Now what, has he run out of tea?"

"Don't ask me. I'm just the messenger." He turned away and started back down the hill.

The next day, Tangar stood over his father in the clearing of the elder's tent. "I have to go fetch some useless herbs for Molar so I'll be back in a week or two. I wanted to ask you to not – upset Tarann while I'm gone. I know you're just trying to help, but she's sensitive about the baby and doesn't really appreciate what you say. OK?"

Thoma thoughtfully moved an icon on his prayer circles. "Herbs of wisdom guide on."

"Yeah, he could use some wisdom. He called it trancon and gave me this guide stick."

Thoma studied the crooked little wand and began rummaging through his medicine pouch. He untied the medicine cloth, sorted through a bundle of guide sticks, and pulled one free handing it to him. "Tanasin guide on."

"Ah, yeah, I don't think Molar would like it much if I don't get the herb he wants. He's out of torish root and is looking for something stronger."

The old man took his talking stick in hand and traced along its length. "Know beyond the guide stone for the little man foretold."

Tangar clutched both guide sticks in his left hand and noticed that they were very similar. "You want me to find some tanasin for the boy? I don't think it's a very good idea to give him spirit herbs."

He tapped repeatedly on a particular bump on his talking stick. "Climb, climb, climb oh children of Shanare. Seek the wisdom of the little man."

"OK... What's that silly song got to do with anything? Look, do we have a deal? You stay away from Tarann until I get back, and I'll find your herb for you."

By the second day of his journey, he realized that, in spite of the marked difference in craftsmanship, both guide sticks led along the same path. He noted that the tanasin stick was slightly longer with an ornate twist at the end, but it would be of no importance for several more days.

In a little over a week, he found the trancon Molar had demanded and finally considered the tanasin stick his dad had given him. It showed another couple of days walk and then he would have to figure out what the crooked little twist on the end was all about.

While the walk had been challenging in places, it wasn't strenuous. He knew he could easily reach the goal described by the stick but he missed Tarann and worried about her. The question of doing his father's bidding over the comfort of his wife's charms lingered at his evening meal. *If I hadn't bargained with Dad I could consider my job done and head home with Molar's herb, but then I'll have to tell Pop I forgot about his. He'll never believe that. Crap! How do I get myself into these things? I'm stuck doing the bidding of a fool and a crazy old man.*

As he drifted off to sleep, he caught a glimpse of Chilbain sitting by the fire with his weapons at the ready. It was a sobering recognition that being alone on the grassy plain was a dangerous proposition that he was taking too lightly. "So old friend, you visit me now to tell me again of my folly in doing Molar's bidding."

The remainder of the night was a fitful vigil of tending the fire with his spear at the ready. A pack of dogs near dawn confirmed the concern of the specter. They were easily dealt with but the appearance of his faithful companion seemed to mock his disregard for customary hunting rules. "It's good to see you old friend, but I hope I'm not disturbing your rest with my foolishness."

Upon returning to the lakeside village, he could hardly wait to tell Tarann of his adventure. The escapade of fetching the tanasin herb for his father still haunted him. *I'll have to scold Dad for being so vague about what to expect. That crook on the end of the guide stick took two extra days to figure out and ended in a damn tough climb. I almost fell twice and then discovering that spooky old temple really set the scene for a disturbing spirit walk. I had to be sure I had the right plant, but now I doubt I can convince anyone of what I saw.*

As he approached the closed door of his hut, he was shocked to see wilted flowers strewn across the path. He now understood why Lambert seemed so guarded when he dropped the trancon herbs off at Molar's. He burst through the door. "What's happened? What's going on?"

Caran knelt at Tarann's bed swabbing her brow while Charona tended kitchen duties at the fire. "She lost the baby, but she's getting better now."

He quickly knelt with her, pulling her close. "Dear God have mercy on her."

Her eyes fluttered open sleepily. "I'm OK, but – I lost our baby. I'm so sorry." She started to cry.

"It's OK. As long as you're all right. That's all I care about. That's all that matters."

She retched violently into a nearby bowl. "No! No, it's not! My baby's gone... Don't you understand? Don't you care? I hate you. You don't care about my baby." She retched again and rubbed her mouth roughly. "The women are right. I'm too old. I'm sorry... I'm so sorry."

"Hush. Don't talk of such things. They're just jealous of you. You're not too old. You'll see. We'll have our baby when the time's right."

"It's your father's curse. I was fine until he cursed me." She again retched into the bowl, broke into tears, and wouldn't be consoled.

"It's Molar's fault. I should've been here for you. If he hadn't sent me looking for his damn herbs, I could've helped." The tanasin root in his pocket tugged at his thoughts. *If I hadn't spent the extra time on Dad's stupid quest I might've been able to save him, or was it a her? It doesn't matter. I wonder where it is? Have they burned it already? These aren't questions for Tarann. Perhaps they aren't questions for anyone. I'm too sad to think straight.*

Tarann nodded off to sleep in his arms. She had obviously been given a sleeping potion. "What have you given her?"

Caran gestured to the nearby table. "Just tea from the master. He said it would help her rest."

Tangar sniffed at the muddy brown brew. "How long has she been drinking this?"

"I don't know. A little over a week, I guess. She wasn't feeling well so Molar gave her this to help her rest. It seemed to work, but then the baby came. Since then, it is the only way she'll rest."

Tangar's hand shook with rage as he carried the cup of tea to Molar's tent. Lambert was preoccupied with Maron so he easily pushed past them at the door and threw the cup in Molar's face. "You've killed my child, you bastard and now I'm going to kill you!"

Lambert recovered quickly and grabbed him from behind.

Molar wiped his face casually. "How dare you accuse me? I've killed no one, least of all a baby. There must be some misunderstanding. Children are a most precious gift. I would never do such a thing."

"You gave her rose-blood tea. You knew that it would kill the baby."

"Yes, I gave her tea. She came to me and asked for something to sooth her. She didn't tell me she was with child. How was I to know?"

"You should've asked. A good Seer knows to ask these things."

"I asked if she knew of anything bothering her and she said only the curse of your father. So perhaps you should talk with him... Take him away." Molar waved dismissively to Lambert.

"This isn't over."

"Yes, I'm afraid it is. Unless, of course, you'd like to explain why that old fool is cursing people with his blasphemous nonsense. The high council doesn't take kindly to that sort of thing. They'll put him away for sure."

Tangar paced deliberately across the commons and approached the elders' hut. He didn't really have a plan but he wanted to strike out at someone or something. "Pop, I need to talk to you."

Thoma considered his son's tone. "Speak wisely."

"Tarann lost the baby. She blames you. She thinks you cursed her."

Thoma stared silently at the prayer circles before him for several moments. "There's no wisdom in this. The child could not be, for the Keeper must come in time."

"See, that's what I'm talking about. I don't understand what you're talking about. Tarann doesn't understand. It scares her, and now this loss plagues her soul. She blames herself – I blame myself. I should've been here for her. I shouldn't have gone looking for your stupid herbs. She let Molar poison her. He killed the baby with rose-blood and now she can't sleep without it. What am I to do?"

"Tanasin, spirit walks with guide of knowledge."

"Tanasin? What's that got to do with anything? My son's been murdered, and all you can think about is your damn weed! What's wrong with you? If you hadn't sent me on that wild goose chase I would've been here for her."

"The grace of Vau prepares the temple. Find wisdom in Her ways."

"Temple? What kind of crap is that? I'm talking about my wife. She's nearly ruined and all you can do is quote some vague crap from the scrolls. Don't you care about her, about me, at all?"

"Spirit walks in wisdom of sky-temple."

"More scrolls... Look, I know you think you're making sense, but I don't understand. You send me to that weird place to fetch some useless weed while my wife is being drugged. How am I to deal with that? I nearly broke my neck getting up that cliff and all you have to say is a bunch of crap from those damn scrolls. How am I to cope? How am I...? How?"

Thoma's eyes misted as he gazed upon his son's anguish. He reached out to place his hand on his head and began to chant softly. "Climb, climb, climb oh children of Shanare..."

The song from his childhood echoed in his ears as visions of the eerie 'sky-temple' flashed across his mind. It had seemed so important to him when he discovered it and now it didn't matter at all. It was just like the sacred scrolls, just another distraction from real life. "OK – we're getting off the subject. Look Pop, you have to stop talking about the Keeper and all that stuff. Molar says he's going to have you put away if you don't stop scaring people."

"Molar fears knowledge. The Keeper comes to hold the way safe from fear. Tanasin guides the man foretold."

"Not that again. Look, I told you. Chilcoat's too young. I'll not allow him to take spirit herbs. Besides, he wants no part in being a Seer. He's a hunter like his father and sees no good in the ways of potions and chants."

"He sees his part well enough. Spirit herbs are for those that don't see as well."

"OK. Look, do you understand what I'm saying? No more 'Keeper' or 'man foretold' around Tarann, and stay clear of Molar. Just keep everything quiet for a while. OK?"

"Secret of sky-temple."

"Yeah, keep that place quiet too. Here, take this and don't do anything stupid with it." Tangar reluctantly dug the tanasin root from his pocket and handed to the old man.

Thoma gazed at the form of the "little man" for a moment and placed it carefully in the embers. "Spirit of Shanare rests."

Tangar resisted the urge to retrieve his hard-fought trophy. "Well, I guess that's fitting. I'll be seeing you Pop. You stay out of trouble."

Caran and Charona were coyly teasing Chilcoat when he arrived home. "You three break it up. Caran I think Pop will need you soon and you should get some firewood before it gets dark."

Chilcoat didn't like being ordered around and having the girls present somehow made it worse. "I'll get to it. I'm busy."

"Hmm... How's your mother?"

"My mother's dead..." He snapped and then reconsidered his reply. "She's getting better, I think. She asked about you."

"Good. Now you three tend to your duties and stop this child's play."

After another few moments of awkward silence, the girls bid farewell and went about their day. Tangar went quietly to Tarann's side. "How are you? Is there anything I can get you?"

"I'm – shaky. Tea would help."

"Hmm, yes that's a good idea. Maybe some cochin would be good." He began sorting through his herbs.

"Will it help me sleep?"

"No. I think you've slept enough for now. I think you should move around a little."

"No. I want to sleep. I need to sleep."

"You'll feel better once you've had some tea."

"I don't want to feel better. I want my baby. I want to forget that any of this happened."

"I understand, but the tea Molar gave you isn't good for you. It'll keep you from getting better."

"It helps me forget. That's what I want... I want to forget." Her hand trembled as she placed it gently on a tightly wrapped bundle at her side. "It's not fair. Why has this happened to me? Why has God given me this child and then taken him away? Am I so wicked that I don't deserve my baby? Why has your father cursed me?"

"He didn't. He wouldn't. He was just trying to explain his readings of the scrolls. He didn't mean to upset you."

"Then why has this happened? What have I done to deserve this?"

Her questioning of God's wisdom grated hard on his commitment. All of his training, all of his knowledge, rested heavily on an unquestioning faith that YodHeaVau loved him and would only do what is best for him and his loved ones but Molar's role in sending him away and prescribing rose tea lingered in his thoughts. *Why would Vau let him take my son? What purpose could it possibly serve to take such an innocent? Dogma is no answer. None of what I've learned answers such questions. How am I to profess knowledge to combat her disbelief when I have such doubts?*

His mind raced but found no good answer. All he could think of was platitudes from too much time spent studying worthless rags. "Only Vau knows. We must have faith that She has done the right thing. She knew the baby was sick. She has taken what is Hers and given him a new life."

"Here, drink this tea and I'll take care of this." He placed his hand on hers, gently pulling the bundle away.

She resisted and broke into tears as he insisted. "Tarance," her hand quaked as she relinquished control.

"Tarance… That's a fine name for my son. I'll remember him always."

With the bundle held carefully before him, he moved to the lakeshore, set the bundle aside, and gathered wood. Taking a good stout branch, he began drawing a large prayer symbol in the sand.

Friends and neighbors soon gathered to watch as he built a neat stack of wood in the center of the diagram. They whispered of possible retribution for his blasphemous actions and guardedly watched his resurrection of the old ceremony.

"Chilc, go tell Caran to bring my father and see if your mother is ready."

Chilcoat nearly carried Tarann the last few feet as she realized what was happening. The bundle lay solemnly atop the neatly stacked tower of wood. She broke into tears again and couldn't be consoled.

Tangar pulled her close into the circle of Vau and gestured to the circle of Yod. "Father if you would please stand as the rightful Seer of this clan, and Chilcoat, if you would do the honor of Hea's last breath."

He handed him a lit torch and gestured for him to stand in the circle of Hea.

Thoma released his hold on Caran and tottered to stand in his place. She quickly sought the comfort of her sister standing nearby in the growing crowd of onlookers. The scene took on an aura of defiance that she feared would somehow blame her for what had happened.

Thoma had only his talking stick to act as a scepter, but he held his head high, scanned his wand across the gathering crowd, and spoke clearly. "This child, Tarance, has been taken before his time but lives on forever in the hearts of his family. Hail YodHeaVau. Whisper ever gently on his soul."

As was the custom of the old ways, Tangar began a mournful funerary chant that cut through the evening air in clear unrestrained tones. Tarann wept uncontrollably as several of the older folks in the crowd joined in the second verse.

Chilcoat looked nervously at Tarann and carefully placed the torch at the base of the tower. The flames soon consumed the precious bundle and dwindled to a meager flicker at the water's edge.

By now, Molar stood judgmentally watching the ceremony. The crowd quickly dispersed fearing retribution for their involvement. "You condemn the child to damnation because you're too proud to admit that I am the rightful Seer of this clan. This will not go unpunished."

Tangar knelt at the fire, took a handful of ashes and pressed a single handprint on his chest. "You're right. My son's death is on your head and will not be forgiven."

Tarann wiped the tears from her face and lowered her hand slowly into the ashes. Her hand quivered as she pulled it slowly away and stared at the smudge where the tears had mixed with the ashes. The world stopped for her. She couldn't move. She couldn't breathe.

Tangar reached slowly to take her hand and comfort her.

She snatched it away from him and held the treasure to her chest rocking silently. The smudge burned a hole in her heart as she held her baby one last time.

Tarann's recovery progressed slowly through the summer. Physically she was well enough to do her work, but emotionally she continued to slip in and out of fits of depression. When things were good, she cheerfully went about her business and mothered Chilcoat only good-naturedly. When things were bad, she would do no more than lie in bed and cry.

On one of the better days, Chilcoat strode proudly across the village commons wielding his father's spear. He wanted to practice with his dad's bow, but found it still too difficult to draw. In his frustration, he grabbed his spear and hefted its weight. *It's heavy, but manageable.*

Tarann was working at the central hearth with several other women as Chilcoat passed. "Ah, good, you're here. Go fetch my purse from the tent."

"I'm busy. Can't you see I'm going hunting?"

She hated to press him, but she knew she would soon need her womanly things. "It'll only take you a moment. Do it for your old mom."

The other women snickered slightly as he struggled to gain some respect. "You're not my mom... I'm busy."

The sting of his retort echoed harshly in her ears. She had been casually joking with the other women about motherly duties and wasn't prepared for such a public rebuke. "Go then! Don't listen to me. Don't do what you're told you ungrateful child."

She quickly gathered her things and left the clutch of women in a swirl of smoke from the morning fire. Tears brimmed in her eyes as she hurried into the tent. She couldn't allow the other women know how hurt she was. The familiar pain in her chest returned as she curled up on her bed and wept. The loss of Tarance ripped at her again with the realization that she wasn't Chilcoat's mother. She wasn't anyone's mother.

Tangar found her inconsolable. "Now what's happened?"

"Nothing, leave me alone."

"Again, 'nothing'... If it's nothing, then stop crying and get to work."

"He's an ungrateful brat! I want him to apologize."

"I assume we're talking about Chilcoat."

"Yes. He embarrassed me in front of the other women. They laughed at me. I want him to say he's sorry in front of everyone."

"Hmm, yes. I'll go tell him that he needs to apologize."

"No! He should think of it himself. It's no good if he doesn't feel it."

"He's a boy. He doesn't feel anything except hunger. How about if I take him hunting for a few days. I'll talk to him about it and it'll give you a chance to forgive him."

"That's your answer for everything? You leave me alone and wander around in the woods smoking herbs and I'm supposed to forgive him."

"I'm just saying, maybe we should give it some time to settle out. You know, he has his own problems with growing up and all."

"You always take his side. Well, go. Both of you get out of here. I don't care if you ever come back."

He found Chilcoat at the practice range ineffectually jabbing the bull with his father's spear. "I doubt he's going to stand still while you do that."

"What? Oh, yeah, I was just seeing if I could – never mind. I suppose you're going to yell at me."

"Why would I do that?"

"I know. I shouldn't have snapped at – Mom. It's just sometimes she acts like I'm her servant or something. I mean, I'm practically grown up and she still treats me like I'm a little kid."

"Don't rush it. You want so badly to be older while I wish I were young again. You'll always be her little kid. It's the way mom's are."

"She's not my mom."

"She is, and you should recognize that. You can go around with a chip on your shoulder about what happened, or you can grow up and accept it."

"How am I supposed to accept my mom dying?"

"Look around. Look at the men at the dawn watch. All of them have lost their mothers. It's part of life. I know you've had it rough because your mom died so young, and maybe that means you feel it more than the men that watch over the village, but they feel it too. They just know there's nothing they can do about it but shed a tear and move on."

"Move on... That's the best advice you have?"

"I can quote scripture. Would you rather hear that? You want so badly to be a man. That's the only advice there is for a man. You can sit around and feel sorry for yourself, or you can get on with life and do something about it. Ask yourself, what would a man do? What would your dad do?"

"What about her? When's she going to move on? I feel like I have to walk on eggshells around her. That's not the way a mom should be."

"I see. Have you told her this? I mean, perhaps you're a better mother than she is and she could benefit from your wisdom."

"You know what I mean. You're the same way. Everyone treats her like some kind of princess or something."

"Hmm, yes, I just had this same conversation with her and she told me to get lost too. I'm beginning to think I'm not very good at this sort of thing. Well, come on. We're going hunting. You want to bring that lance or would you rather have something more fitting?"

"Yeah, I guess."

"Good, that's what a man would do. Recognize your limitations and work to overcome them."

"Sounds like a bunch of crap from your scrolls."

"Ha! I can't get anything past you."

Tarann was correct. No sooner had Tangar and Chilcoat left than she began her womanly cycle. The discomfort mounded upon the loneliness and regret she felt about her last exchange with both men. She muttered to herself. "So Vau, You plague me with this unseemly reminder that I'm yet but a woman, but You deny me the child that is my due."

This line of thinking, of course, led to thoughts of Tarance, which made the discomfort worse. *At least then, I had Molar's tea to drive the wretchedness away.*

She resolved to seek out the other women that were also afflicted. They gathered in the women's tent, worked diligently weaving intricate lace fabric, and gossiped incessantly to sooth their nerves. They understood her conflict with Chilcoat better than she herself would admit and gave her words of encouragement.

On the third day of her vigil Molar came by to check up on their wellbeing. The Seer was required to make these occasional rounds to dispense what aid he could to make their lives less difficult. His eyes fell on Tarann as if a game piece had just fallen into place. "Tarann, how are you? Is there anything I can do for you?"

"No. I'm fine."

"I hope you don't mind my saying, but, you don't look fine. Here, let me get you something." He called Maron close and whispered to her. She quickly left and returned in a few minutes with a small jug.

Tarann immediately recognized the muddy brown tea. "Ah, no thanks, I don't need anything."

Molar pressed the pot into her hand. "Please take it. You may find it a comfort tonight when you're alone. I want you to know that you can count on me for comfort in your time of loss. I'm so sorry for any misunderstanding we may have had. I want to assure you that I have your best interest at heart."

The other women watched the transaction with little concern. They all had taken relief from Molar's remedies from time-to-time.

As evening set in, the comfort of the women's camaraderie faded and their relentless chatter grew tiresome. Tarann carefully gathered her patches of lace and guardedly stashed the pot of tea amongst her things for the return home.

She sat alone at her hearth prodding the fire and wondered when Tangar and 'the boy' would return. She envied Tangar's ability to simply smoke his herbs and consider forgiveness in the name of God. She couldn't bring herself to give over to a god that had treated her so unfairly. A particularly vicious cramp seized her as she whispered. "My precious Tarance, I'm so sorry that I am so unfit."

As she curled up on her bed and began to cry, she noticed the tea Molar had given her. Moving the pot closer to the fire to warm it, she considered a scrap of bread to settle her stomach. After several minutes of unrestrained weeping, she sat up cross-legged, dried her face, and nibbled at the crust of dry bread.

She was surprised that Molar had sweetened the tea with honey. The nectar coated her throat and settled quietly in her stomach as a warm glow. Sipping slowly at the cup, she savored the flush that spread up her chest and along her arms. The cramps were gone. The pain was gone. The concern with the brash young boy was gone.

After several minutes, she realized that her cup of tea had gone cold, not just tepid, but completely cold. It came as a flash, as if she had just awakened. The sudden focus of reality soon faded to a distant scene of herself viewed from across the room. As she took a sip of the cold tea, a familiar haze swept over her. She had grown to love its warm embrace and now it seemed even more precious to her. A young boy came and sat next to her by the fire. He was near Chilcoat's age, strong and slender, not stout like Chilcoat. She knew he was Tarance. She could feel his warm loving presence. He smiled and tried to play a small flute. She guided his hand gently to find the soft pure notes.

As the morning light crept across her hand, she realized that she still held the half-empty cup of rose tea. She hadn't moved from her place by the hearth. The fire had long since gone cold and her legs were stiff from sitting cross-legged all night. She gazed into the muddy brown liquid and carefully put it aside.

The pang of cramps told her to attend to her condition. Her limbs were heavy as she shuffled through her morning duties. By midday, she had accomplished everything she needed to do and sat at her hearth wondering when Tangar would return. *I hope he's not hurt.*

She turned to the pot of tea, measured out what remained into her cup, and sat looking at it. It was cold but, sniffing at it, she could almost taste the honey. She sipped the tiniest sample and let it trickle down her throat. Her cramps soon diminished and her concern for Tangar lost out to her estimating how long the remaining tea would last.

The next morning, she went through the now familiar ritual of regaining consciousness. She gazed blankly into the empty teacup and tried to remember if she had somehow spilled it. The ghost of Tarance had again visited her lonely night with a pleasant tune he had learned. The warmth of the memory swept over her and she couldn't help but smile at the love she felt.

When, at last, she finished her morning routine she settled at her hearth and considered her condition. The cramps were nearly gone but she needed another day's worth of tea to be sure. *I so want to see Tarance again.*

Soon she stood at Molar's door. "...and so, if you wouldn't mind, I'd appreciate enough of that sweet tea to get me through another day."

Maron gave the slightest smirk. "Sure, I understand. Come in. I'll see what I can do."

"Here's your jug." Tarann dug the pot out of her purse.

After a few moments Molar appeared in the doorway of his room. He was wearing his wrinkled ceremonial robe and nothing else. "So, you need some more huh? I thought you might like that. I'll be glad to let you have some but I need something in return. I'm afraid I'm going to have to send your husband out to gather some more herbs soon. Where is he anyway? I haven't seen him around lately."

"He's hunting. He'll be back soon."

"Well, that's good. Wouldn't want to leave a woman alone too long. No telling what might happen." He took the jug and filled it from a large pot he pulled from a shelf. The process only took a moment, but he managed to allow his robe to gap open while he juggled the vessels.

"Here you go. You let me know if there's anything else I can do for you."

Tangar and Chilcoat dragged a hastily constructed skid down the main path into the village. A large buck straddled the poles in a somewhat gruesome display of hunting prowess. They stopped at the central hearth and bartered with the grandmothers over the disposition of the hide. With a deal struck, they quickly availed themselves of a well-earned bath in the lake.

Chilcoat spotted Caran in the bean field and quickly went to greet her. Tangar scanned the work parties in the gardens but didn't find Tarann. *She must be weaving,* he thought.

Throwing the door open to his hut, he expected a warm greeting. The scene shocked him. Tarann lay unconscious on a crumpled pile of bedding. An empty jar lay on the floor near the cold fire pit.

He ran to her and was relieved to find her still warm. *She's only vaguely responsive, but at least, she's alive.* Picking up the jar, he sniffed at it. "Damn him... Tarann, can you hear me? Tarann! Listen to me. You need to wake up. Tarann..." He jostled her repeatedly.

"Lv me lone. I wnta slp."

"You need to wake up. Come on. Sit up. I'll make some tea." He propped her up against a roll of bedding and started collecting kitchen utensils scattered about the room.

She leaned slowly toward the bed with her eyes still closed. "Slp."

"No. No sleep. Wake up!" He filled a pot with water and turned to consider the cold fire pit. Tarann tried in vain to pull bedding over her head. "Oh no you don't." He poured the pot of cold water over her head.

"Ah! Stop." She sputtered and swung weakly at the stream.

"Wake up, or I'll go get more."

"Wa's wrng wit you? I needta rest."

"You've rested enough. Where did you get this?" He held up the teapot.

She squinted past a tangle of dripping red hair. "Molr"

"Why? Why did he give you this?"

"I – I'm – sick. I need help."

"What do you mean, 'sick'? What's wrong with you?"

"My – baby's gone. It brngs Trnce back to me. I cn't stand it. I can't... 'snot fair."

"OK. I understand, but you can't drink this stuff. It'll make a slave of you."

"You dn't ndrstnd... You can't... You're not a mther... I just wanta frget... I needta frget bout my baby – bout Tarance. I needta frget bout you... You needta frget bout me."

"I don't want to forget about you. I don't want to forget about Tarance. He's part of my life and I love him. I love you. Vau will take my memories soon enough. Until then, I want to remember every moment. Yes, there's pain; more pain than I want. Perhaps, more pain than is fair but the pain belongs to me. It makes me who I am. It's part of me."

She sat silently collecting her thoughts for several moments. "Oh, so noble... Well, I'm not. I'm just a simple woman. I'm not even a woman. I can't even give you the son you deserve."

"I have a son. He is the man foretold. I can ask for nothing more."

"He's not my son. He hates me."

"He doesn't hate you. He loves you. He's just afraid it disrespects Catherin."

"I take nothing from Catherin. I just want him to give me some of what God refuses me. I – I can't help it."

"God refuses you nothing. It's written that you'll be the mother of the man foretold and the keeper of the word."

"Don't! Don't you dare curse me with your witch's tale and your father's games. I'll not have it! I'd rather be barren than burden my children with such nonsense."

"I understand. I too wish it could be other than what it is. I've puzzled over the scrolls for years now and I find no other way to read them. I'm sorry."

"No. No, you're not. You like the vision you've conjured. You wish this tragedy on your children. You take advantage of a grief-stricken boy to play at being a father. Well, you're not. You're an impotent pretender to the Seer's robes. And, now you deny me the comfort I need from the real Seer. Well, I've had enough of your pretense and games. I'll drink my tea and I'll forget. It's as it should be."

"No! You're my wife, and you'll do as I say. I'll not allow you to waste your life dreaming forgotten dreams. This tea will kill you, just as it killed our baby. Molar is evil and certainly not the real Seer. He should've never given you this poison. A real Seer would know better. He wants you dependent on his drugs so that you'll not question his corruption."

"At least, I understand his ways. He doesn't hide behind scrolls no one understands and silly games conjured up by some old fool that doesn't make any sense. His ways are simple. I do what he asks, and he provides what I need. No chanting to a god that hates me."

"God doesn't hate you. He loves you so much He's given you this special task. He knows you're the person that'll do what's right. He knows only you are strong enough to raise two such special people."

She pulled her wet hair back in a rope over her shoulder. "You make my head hurt and my skin crawl."

"It's Molar's tea. Come on, we'll go for a swim. That'll help wash away some of the effects."

The pair soon sat clean and dressed by their now glowing hearth. Chilcoat appeared with the freshly butchered hindquarter from the buck they had provided. He presented it to Tarann as if it were a ceremonial offering. "I'm sorry if I seemed harsh the other day. It's just sometimes, I feel like – like you treat me like a little kid. So I brought you this to say I'm sorry."

"That's not necessary. Tangar's share will keep us."

Tangar lit his pipe and sat back watching the exchange. "I have no share. Chilcoat took this kill singlehanded. I did nothing more than help carry it."

"Well, then I'm grateful that you... I'm grateful that you live here. I'm sorry if I treat you like a child. You are my child. I've watched you grow from nothing more than a slip of a bird with a broken wing to a man that doesn't need a mother anymore. I'm sorry, but I still need my little boy. The little boy that used to cry on my shoulder when he skinned his knee. I can't help it. It's the way I feel."

"I know, and I still need you. I cry often enough. Now it's not as often for a skinned knee but for you... I don't mean to hurt you."

She pursed her lips and looked to Tangar. "Did you put him up to this?"

"I had nothing to do with it. We spoke only of hunting and other manly things."

She gave him a sideways glance. "Manly things like apologizing for being a man?"

"It's a fine art. Now, I have to go check on Pop. Anyone want to come?"

"... So Pop, I was thinking that maybe it's time for you to stay at the gathering village. Some of your old friends are there. It might be fun for you."

Thoma sat at his usual place rearranging various trinkets on the prayer circles. "Fun to awaken…"

Tangar was relieved that he seemed to be coherent. "Yeah, I know what you mean, but you wouldn't have to make the long walk back. That's something isn't it? I mean, you always seem to have a hard time getting over Lion's Pass."

"What of the Keeper? I'm to meet the Keeper before I die."

"Who said anything about dying? I'm just saying that it might be good for you to stay, that's all."

"The woman weeps of change."

"Yeah, you know how it is. Speaking of which, do you know of a cure for rose poisoning?"

Thoma's face grew solemn. "Wisdom of time." He began rummaging through his pouch and grumbling to himself. The grumble grew more rhythmic as he extracted the bundles of guide sticks. By the time he had sorted them and selected a twig the grumbling had turned into a chant that dwelt on the folly of the rose.

Tangar was amazed that, while his voice wasn't pure and clear as it once had been, he didn't falter on any of the words. "You remember the song well."

Thoma seemed not to notice that he was chanting as he handed the twig to him. "Guide on temple."

"Temple? This is a winter herb. Will it cure rose poisoning?"

"Wisdom of time sooths what cannot be cured."

"That doesn't sound very good, especially if I have to wait until we get to the temple. Isn't there anything else?"

"Vau's craving for the Keeper."

"That'll be a hard sell. You're going to have to show me all that 'Keeper' stuff in the scrolls if I'm ever going to be able to convince anyone."

Thoma gazed back upon his prayer circles and moved an icon imperceptible toward the center. "Yod reveals all in its time."

"Yeah, speaking of time, you need to start getting ready for the gathering journey. I'd like to get an early start this time. We missed the opening ceremonies last year."

***

The early start allowed Thoma to doddle even more than usual so they still managed to miss the opening ceremony.

Tarann's disappointment was rooted more in her contempt for Thoma than her desire to see the ceremony. "He did it on purpose. He always does something to make us late."

Tangar listened halfheartedly while he continued to erect their tent. "Yeah, I suppose it gives him a feeling of power, like he's still important. Don't worry about it. He's gone to the elder's lodge now."

Her resentment of the old man's manipulations wouldn't allow her to let the subject go. "I've been trapped with that old fool for weeks now and I need to tell someone about it, and since you're not listening to me... never mind. I'm going to find some – pepper. We're out."

Tangar looked up from his toil with little regard for her tirade. "See if you can find some morning tea while you're at it."

She soon found her way to the market stalls and secured an ample supply of staples. Despite being among old friends bartering over the quality of various items, her mood remained aggravated. The sunlight seemed harsh and the shopkeepers seemed unreasonably firm about their prices.

As she packed up her last item, Maron appeared at her side making a pretense of interest in the price she had paid. "You drive quite a bargain. I see you found a good strong tea. That should get you going."

Tarann nervously shuffled packages and tried to be civil. "Yes, it's from the central highlands."

"Is it? Well perhaps we can share a cup some day."

"Yes. That would be nice."

"I know. I have some tea already made. Why don't you come with me and we'll have a cup and talk. I haven't seen you much lately."

"Ah, nah, that's alright. I have to get back." She hefted her load of packages.

"Oh, I insist. You can spare a couple of minutes. Here, I'll help carry some of this." She grabbed at one of the smaller packets.

Tarann snatched the parcel away. "Ah, please. I need to get going."

"Molar was asking about you the other day. He's worried that perhaps you still need some – consolation after your horrible ordeal. He's very concerned that you're not getting the correct treatment."

The itch on the back of her neck crawled into her spine causing her shoulders to tighten and her head to twist tightly to the left. "I'm fine, really."

Maron reached quickly into her purse, extracted a small pouch, and stuffed it in amongst Tarann's packages. "Well, here, Molar asked me to give you this. It's only enough for a couple of cups, but it should help you feel better. Put a little honey in it to take the bitterness out."

Tarann flushed with alarm. "Ah, no, that's alright. I really can't take it."

Maron smiled slightly and turned to go. "Let me know when you need more."

Tarann juggled her packages awkwardly. The packet nestled deeper into the load as Maron disappeared into the crowd. Relief swept over her as she realized the confrontation was over and she had the packet of contraband intact.

She felt dirty at the realization that her main concern was with the tea. She knew she should throw it away, but its comforting glow lingered in her thoughts. The familiar craving tugged at her gut and the ants on the back of her neck danced in anticipation.

Tangar had finished with the tent and was unloading the last of the household goods when she arrived. "Ah, good you're back. Did you find everything you wanted?"

"Yes," was all she could think to say as she went to work arranging her home.

Stafon and Talbot stood at the edge of Tangar's newly claimed clearing. "It's about time you showed up. We missed you at the opening ceremony."

"Yeah, you know how the old man is. We're lucky we got here at all. I thought Tarann was going to strangle him. So what have you two been up to without me?"

Stafon moved a log to use as a chair. "Big changes here. Nolan buckled under to the pressure and joined the enlightened. That makes old Talbot here Bishain's Number One."

Tangar dropped a large stone near the fire pit. "Really? Congrats old man. I knew you could do it."

Talbot put his foot on the stone while Tangar backfilled with dirt. "It's not official or anything. Bishain just sort of doesn't include Nolan anymore."

Tangar nudged another large stone toward the hearth. "What does that do to our studies?"

Talbot again put his foot on the stone. "That's why we're here. We're going to have to be careful. I have the scrolls put away so they're safe for now, but we have to be sure none of Stanton's boys get wind of what we're doing."

Tangar grunted. "Is it really that bad? I mean, we're just reading some dusty old rags. Who cares?"

Stafon lit his pipe. "Stanton... He thinks it's an insurrection challenging his insurrection."

Tangar sat on one of the stones. "Forget him. I want my dad to look at the scrolls. He claims there's something about my kids in there and I want him to show me. It's a big issue with Tarann that I'd like to put behind us."

Stafon chocked on his pipe. "What kids?"

"That's just it. He claims the scrolls say I'm to be the father of 'the man foretold' and 'the keeper of the word' and Tarann hates him for it. I just want to see what he's talking about so I can calm her down. She thinks he cursed her and that's why she lost our baby."

Stafon coughed and spit. "Ah, geeze, sorry to hear about that. I know Tarann really wants a kid."

Tangar looked toward the tent and lowered his voice. "Yeah. I think Molar poisoned her. He gave her rose-blood tea and then she lost the baby."

Stafon blew through his pipe to clear it. "Rose-blood! Why would he do that? That stuff can really mess you up."

"He claimed he didn't know… It doesn't matter. He did it and we lost the baby. It's done now. I just want to move on, and the best way I can think to do that is to find the stuff Dad's talking about in the scrolls and tell her what it really means."

Talbot remained with his foot on a stone. "All I'm saying is, we need to be careful or Stanton will take the scrolls for safekeeping and we'll never see them again."

Tangar dressed in his best hunting garb and clutched at his spear. "I'm going to go get my butt kicked at the spear throw. You want to come and watch?"

Tarann sat by the morning fire gazing into the meager flame. "No. I'm tired. I'll just take a little nap."

He was disappointed that she seemed so downhearted. *She's normally so happy to finally get to the gathering and see old friends. I hope she snaps out of it soon.*

She continued her vigil for several minutes. When she was sure he was gone, she dug into her cooking provisions and extracted the tea Maron had given her. Clutching the packet secretively in her fist, she peeked out the door to be sure she was alone. The warmth of the moment quickly lost out to memories of the last time she had used it. *Tangar had been so harsh. He doesn't understand. He doesn't miss Tarance the way I do. He doesn't mourn as he should.*

Carefully metering the powder into a cup, she added hot water and honey.

Savoring the light floral smell for a moment, she quietly sipped at the elixir. The warmth coated the back of her throat and spread down her chest in throbbing acknowledgment of her heartbeat.

The familiar pang of mourning swept over her as she thought of Tarance and things that might have been. As she watched the hypnotic flicker of the flame, a comforting haze soon replaced the pain. Tarance, once again, came and sat next to her. He was older now, a young man, fully grown. He was strong and handsome. She couldn't help but think that any woman would gladly do his bidding.

The embers smoldered into single wisp of white smoke as she focused on the dregs in the bottom of her cup. Quickly gulping the cold residue, she put the cup aside and stirred the fire back to life. The itch in the back of her head slipped into a comforting numbness that allowed her to finish cleaning the hut. On several occasions, she stopped working and retched unproductively as waves of nausea swept over her.

The empty packet of rose tea drew her attention. She treasured it warmly for several moments then, in a flash of guilt, considered throwing it away. She felt that she needed to hide it, but wasn't sure why. The craving pulled at her shamelessly and she knew Tangar would hate her for having it, yet she couldn't bring herself to discard it. She carefully tucked it in amongst her cooking herbs and dressed for the day.

As she wandered across the village commons, she recognized many faces of old friends but couldn't put a name with any of them. She knew she was looking for Tangar, but wasn't sure she really wanted to talk with him. *He'll recognize the tea and be mad. I'd better stay away from him.*

With a revived notion of urgency, she made her way to the elder's lodge. *If I can find Maron before Tangar finishes his games, I'll be OK. I just need to avoid that old fool, Thoma.*

She peeked into the tent in glimpses of exposure around the door curtains. She could see Thoma's bush of wild hair surrounded by a small group of onlookers, but Maron didn't seem to be among them. She was about to leave when Molar stepped up behind her. "Whom do you seek?"

She spun quickly to face him. "What? Oh, no one, I was just looking."

"Then you've come to the right place. This is the biggest collection of no one's as I've ever seen."

She forced a slight smile. "I'll be going thanks."

He looked skeptically into her eyes and placed his hand on her arm. "You look – troubled. I don't like to see someone so lovely upset. Is there anything I can do for you?"

"No. I'm fine. I was just sort of looking for Maron. She said she might have something for me."

"Yes, she told me of your – mourning. I think I have something that just might make things better. Of course, I'd like something in return."

"What do you mean?"

"Just a little token of appreciation. Nothing of great value. Just something to mark a customary exchange of goods and services."

"Like what?"

He looked around at passerby's and dug into his satchel to extract a tightly bound packet he held in the palm of his hand. "Perhaps a little kiss between old friends."

Her eyes locked on the sachet and everything else faded from view. She stood transfixed for several moments considering the craving that gnawed at her.

He closed his hand around the packet. "Of course, if you'd rather exchange something else, I'm sure we can come to an agreement. Perhaps there's something your husband can do that is worthy of this remedy"

"Like what?"

"Hmm, yes. Perhaps he can fetch more torish-root for me. I've run out and I need to find an alternative soon. I'm sure you understand… In the meantime, here, take this as a gesture of goodwill and, please, let me know if there's anything else I can do for you."

Smirking slightly as she took the packet, he grabbed her arm and pulled her close. She resisted weakly but the warmth of the packet in her hand seemed to drain her resolve as she allowed him to caress her. She felt detached from her body. She could see herself from across the room as his gnarled fingers groped her form without response. She couldn't feel his hands squeezing and fondling. She could only feel the packet she clutched in her hand. It was more important than anything else.

***

Tangar burst into their tent and propped his spear in its place. "Well, that was a complete bust. Stafon didn't even place this year, but Chilcoat won in the junior's. That kid is getting too good for the likes of me."

Tarann sat unmoved near the hearth. Her robes were rumpled and her hair was tangled. An empty cup lay on its side next to the open packet of tea before her. She looked up at him but didn't seem to recognize him.

"What's going on here?"

"Iss nothin. Jss a lil tea. Iss OK. Mron gav me sm tea."

"Maron? What kind of tea?" He picked up the packet and sniffed at it.

"Iss OK. Trnce comes an we tlk."

"No! It's not OK. Don't you see? No. Of course, you don't see anything but this. The drug blinds you. What am I to do? How am I to fight this?"

"Dn't fight. I wanta see my baby. I needta hold him agin."

"Hold him in your heart, not with this. This is wrong..." He clinched the remaining tea into its wrapper and stuffed it into his pocket. "You keep his spirit from the warmth of his sleep with Vau. You don't want to do that do you? He belongs with Her now. She has important things for him to do. She'll not be happy if you pull him from Her arms."

"He's mine. She cn't hve him. He's mine. He's mine..." She began to sob uncontrollably.

Tangar pulled her close and squeezed her tightly until she couldn't breathe. After several moments, she finally stopped weeping and gasped for air. He released her as she struggled to wipe the tears from her face.

"I've dne smethin vry bad. Plse frgive me? I'm sorry."

"Of course, I forgive you. You've done only what any grieving mother would do. I'm sorry that I haven't seen how – sad you are. It's hard for me to know. I mean, I can't feel what you feel. I can't know what it is to be you."

She slowly regained some composure. "I – I got the tea from Molar. He wants you to do something for him now. I'm sorry. I know I shouldn't have, but I – I'm just too weak. I need it. It makes me feel whole. I can feel the warmth of my baby. If I don't have it, I can't think of anything except his warmth and what a bad mother I am."

"Don't worry. I talked to Dad about it and he said there's a treatment here. I'll get some and everything will be better."

"No. No it won't. Don't you see? I don't want a treatment. I just want to forget. I'll live here and you can take a new wife."

"We've been through all of that. I don't want a new wife. I know this is hard for you, but it's important that you're strong."

She struggled listlessly in his arms. "But I'm not strong. I'm not – I'm not anything."

He again squeezed her tightly. "I'll help. We'll all help. I'll get Dad and even Chilcoat can help. You don't need to worry. We'll be here for you."

"What can anyone do? It eats at me. Every time I think it's gone, it comes creeping back. Gnawing at me from the inside, stealing my will."

"It's OK. We'll beat it. Dad said we can beat it with the help of Vau."

"Dad – that old fool is what's wrong. Him and his damn scrolls... He's cursed me."

"OK. OK. I'll go talk to him and get him to explain himself. You'll see, he hasn't cursed you. He's just confused about some old fable. It'll be OK. I'm sure." Kissing her on the forehead, he grabbed his spear, and left.

At the elders tent he spotted his dad at the center of a small group performing a prayer ritual. A couple of the onlookers seemed earnestly interested but Molar stood nearby, in a cluster of the few, mocking his efforts.

Lambert and another guardian blocked Tangar's entry until he put his spear aside. "Hey Pop, can I pull you away for a little while."

Thoma looked up with a self-satisfied smile and tipped over one of the icons in the prayer circles. A low mumble from a couple of the spectators acknowledged his action. "And so it begins."

Molar scoffed at the apparent revelation and looked directly at Tangar. "Don't run off. I have something for you to do."

The package in his pocket tugged at him. "I have better things to do than cater to your whims."

"Your wife wouldn't like to see you dishonored for shirking your obligation to the Seer now would she?"

"My wife is none of your concern. She'll be proud to know I challenge your claim as Seer. You've poisoned her for the last time." He extracted the packet and tossed it into the ceremonial hearth releasing its content. The powder smoldered for a moment and then a cloud of thick white smoke burst forth. Everyone recognized the heavy aroma, moved back from the lingering haze, and looked to Molar for response.

"You dare challenge me? Your wife will suffer greatly for the medicine you just wasted. Everyone has seen your foolish act and will not be a part of your quest for approval."

"My quest is only to provide **my** people with the healing they need, not your hurtful abuse of herbs. They aren't your people, so you care nothing for them. Your drugs enslave and cripple them. The perverse pleasure you get from watching your hypocrisy triumph far outweighs any obligation you feel for these people. They are merely dupes for your amusement. Well, I'll not stand for it any longer. I challenge your authority as Seer of the lakeshore tribe."

"You challenge? You have no right to challenge anyone. I've taken the roll of Seer because your father has proven himself incompetent and, since he trained you, that makes you incompetent. No. Your bungling nearly killed a healthy young girl and now you deny your own wife the herbs she needs to endure your impotence. These are not the ways of a Seer of the new order. These are the ways of ignorant old fools."

"My challenge stands. The high council will decide who is a fool and who the rightful Seer of the lakeshore tribe is."

The crowd mumbled agreement and looked to Nolan, the highest-ranking elder currently present. He grimaced at having to approve the challenge, but had no choice. "So be it. The Council will meet to resolve this at Bishain's convenience."

Talbot grabbed Tangar as he retrieved his spear. "Are you sure you want to do this?"

"Sure, why not? It's the only way to get rid of him without killing him. Come on Pop let's get out of here." Thoma held Tangar's arm for support.

Talbot stood in their path. "I don't know. I think we should talk about it first."

"We? Are you volunteering to help?"

"Yeah, sure, we; you, me, Stafon... We're in this together. I mean, we're supposed to guard the knowledge of the scrolls. That'll be hard to do if you get thrown off the team."

"I know. I just don't know what else to do. I mean, I can't let him get away with it. He almost killed Tarann."

Thoma poked meaningfully at a particular spot on his talking wand. "Truth hidden for the One."

Tangar winced at his distraction. "Hmm, yes. Speaking of truth, can you show me in the scrolls where it talks about the Keeper?"

"Bonding speaks of birth."

"Bonding? You mean it's in the birth scroll? Well that explains why I haven't noticed it. We haven't been looking at the birth scroll. We've been concentrating on the forgotten scrolls. Great, as if I don't already have enough to do. How can we get our hands on the birth scroll? I mean, they're going to be using it for the bonding ceremony. It'll be missed if we try to take it."

Thoma rubbed his thumb along the length of his wand. "Wisdom of age."

Talbot considered the old man. "I think Bishain has the old copy. He put it aside after the last transcription. I think he's afraid they've copied it incorrectly. The observing elders were of the new order."

Tangar nervously tapped the butt of his spear on the ground. "Is there nothing they haven't tainted? Well, let's go find Stafon. We can get the old copy and Dad can show us what he's talking about."

The reading went predictably slow. Not that Thoma's wanderings slowed them down so much as no one, except Tangar, had much interest in the topic. They had all grown up listening to bits and pieces of the scroll every year at the gathering and, while the unfamiliar parts were of some interest, it just didn't have the intrigue of the forgotten scrolls.

Tangar stopped for the hundredth time. "I don't know Pop. I don't see it. This stuff is just a bunch of rules for newlyweds. I mean, sure, there's some stuff about a 'keeper of the knowledge', but it's all mixed up with a bunch of stuff about Hea bonding with Vau to beget the children of Yod. I don't see anything about a witch and 'the One foretold'."

"Faith of the One."

"See, that doesn't help. How am I to convince Tarann that you're not cursing her when there're things like that all clumped together and all you have to say is 'faith'?"

Stafon shifted uncomfortably and placed a smooth stone on the edge of the scroll where it curled. "This is all very interesting and all, but Laura's going to kill me if I don't get back."

Tangar adjusted the stone slightly. "Liar; I know this stuff is a boring torment for you. I'll let you know if I stumble onto something. Tal, you can leave too. I don't think anything's going to come of this."

Talbot looked up as if from a trance. "Ah, yeah, this quest seems to be going in circles. There is someone called the 'Keeper', or there has been, or there will be, but it's not clear who or when. I guess Thoma's right; all there is, is faith. I'll go see if Bishain has anything to say about it."

"Thanks, I'll see you guys later... Well, Pop, it's just you and me. You want to take a break?"

Thoma watched the two men leave. "Tarann should be here for what I have to say."

Tangar was pleased by his coherence. "Ah, I'm not sure that's such a good idea. She's kind of upset with you right now."

Thoma leaned forward and carefully placed his talking stick under a specific line of text. "The sooner she understands her part, the better it will be for all."

Tangar strained to read the text. *"... the Keeper of the Word and Warrior of Truth."* He handed the stick back and gathered up the document. "OK. Let's take this project to our tent. It's a little more private."

They were about to leave when Thoma stopped and dug into his medicine pouch. "A gift of forgiveness," he answered the unspoken question.

Tarann sat by their hearth mending a small basket. She obviously had not intended to entertain anyone and was upset to have them show up unexpected. Her hair blazed in unforgiving tangles of red profusion where she had obviously been scratching. It gave her a particularly unkempt air. "What are you doing here?"

Thoma spoke before Tangar could deflect her query. "I bring a gift of forgiveness and want only to talk briefly."

She was startled by his clarity. "Gifts aren't necessary. Just state your business and leave."

Thoma nodded his assessment of her condition. "Tea to sooth your spirit." He quickly pulled a small packet from his pouch and went to work brewing a cup of tea for her.

She attempted to pull her hair into some kind of order. "That's not necessary, really."

"Oh, but it is. You see I have things to tell you that will upset you and I want you to listen carefully."

Tangar attempted to defuse the building tension. "Let's just sit and have some tea like a regular family. It's great that Dad has come back to us as his old self. Let's just enjoy it while we can."

"I never left. I smelled the drugs that Stanton tried to give me. He's not nearly as cleaver as he thinks he is. My deception allows me to attend their meetings without suspicion. I'm sorry for the pain it has brought you, both of you, but I assure you it is necessary. It has allowed the truth of the old ways to endure despite their best efforts to kill it. It is the reason you and your friends have been given this task. But I must ask that you keep it secret. My job is still unfinished."

He measured out a large cup of tea for Tarann. "Please drink this and allow me to explain something to you."

She skeptically sipped at the amber liquid. "Aren't you going to have any?"

"No. This brew is for the affliction Molar has given you. I'm sorry that I cannot cure the hunger you have for the rose, but this tonic will lessen the craving for a short time. You must learn to crave life more than his drugs. This will help."

Her eyes filled with tears as she continued to sip at the bitter dregs. "I'm not sure I can do that. My life is without worth. I'm not the wife your son deserves."

"And so now, we'll speak of the scrolls." He grabbed the parchment and spread it on the hearthstone. It took several tries to get it to lie flat, but with the help of her empty cup and an unlit lamp, they smoothed it into place.

"You must understand that what I'm about to tell you is beyond my doing. I am but a messenger. I know you're a very wise woman and wish none of this, but you must understand that you're chosen by YodHeaVau to bring forth the child that will be known as the 'Keeper of the Word and Warrior of Truth'."

He paused to allow her to grasp what he was trying to say.

She looked frightened and confused. "So you do curse me."

After several moments of silence, he finally responded. "Yes, I'm sorry for the pain you are to endure but you are to bear her burden for all the years of your life. She will be a blessing to the people, but she will have many trials to suffer."

He delicately drew his wand along the text. "It says here, 'she will be a witch of great knowledge and wisdom and shall bring forth the one foretold to lead the people in a new world of YodHeaVau's light and grace'."

She stared blankly at the document for a moment and then looked to Tangar. "Are you just going to sit there and let him curse me like that? Curse our daughter like that?"

"Of course not... Now see here Pop. You can't just go and say things like that. I mean, this is all some pretty sketchy stuff here. What makes you think any of this is true or has anything to do with us?"

"I have faith that what is written will come to pass. The man foretold is given to you and your loss of the boy child, Terance, in favor of the Keeper confirms my beliefs. I'm sorry if this seems harsh to you, but it is as written." He stroked the document gently as if to calm it.

Turning to Tarann he held her hand softly. "Rejoice. You are to have the child you prayed for. She will be strong, and healthy, and smart, and loving. She will bring great blessings to our people."

"Blessings, but at what cost? You curse her with unspeakable burdens of witchery and hardship."

"Read the forgotten scrolls. The hardships are to come at the will of Yod. Hea will purge this world of the unworthy so that Vau may bring forth a new cycle of life. Your daughter will be the means for our people to thrive under His new light. This is where the enlightened deceive themselves. They bend this text to suit their purpose and tell themselves they have awoken unto His light, but they haven't. His light is real. It is the means by which He will purge the world of the unworthy. Hea's light will fall upon the face of the earth and the earth will quake from His embrace. Your son, Chilcoat, will lead them through the ordeal and your daughter will bring forth the One who will thrive in this new light so that the children of the Shanare will endure. You can struggle against the will of God and you can hate me for my part in it, but it will not change these things."

Tarann picked up her cup and held it to her chest. "And, what am I to do to bring about this 'blessing'? I am a damaged vessel, forever cursed to crave the embrace of the rose."

Thoma placed the packet of herbs on the scroll. "The kasis vine grows plentifully here at the coast. Your husband knows of its power. It tempers the edge of the rose's thorn. It will become a part of you, – a part of her."

Tangar took his wife's hand. "Yes. Please bond again with me. We can do this if you'll help."

"And you, my son, must continue to learn of the old ways. Teach the child what you learn for she must carry this wisdom."

"Should I not teach these things to Chilcoat? Should he not be the Seer?"

"He'll know the ways of a hunter. He'll be a Seer of great strength and judgment, but he mustn't fall to the lure of herbs to find this wisdom. The witching craft of medicine will fall to the Keeper. She will be the kasis that will temper the seduction of herbs with the spiritual wisdom of YodHeaVau."

Tarann smashed her cup on the hearthstone. "I'll not listen to any more of this. If I'm to have a daughter, she'll not be a part of this mystical nonsense. I'll not have it! She'll be a normal girl, with normal skills, and normal desires, not some witch-shaman."

A slight smile crept onto Thoma's face. "Good, then you do understand. Do your best to raise a woman you can be proud of, but just like any daughter, she will desire to know what her father knows. It's as it should be."

Tangar finished his evening meal with Tarann. From time-to-time, she would start to speak and then stop. "Your father... Your father is a conniving old fox."

"You're too kind."

"Why doesn't he just leave us alone? I mean, if all the stuff he talked about is true, won't it just happen without him being involved?"

"Sure, I guess, in some fashion. Do you want some of your tea?"

She pursed her lips and hesitated for a moment. "No. I'm OK for now. What are you going to do about Molar?"

Grabbing his spear, he started for the door. "I'm going to go talk with him. That's all a civil person can do. I'll convince him to change his ways and leave our tribe for the good of us all."

"Alright, don't tell me. Just don't go getting hurt or worse."

He considered her words and propped his spear in its place with a hint of a smile.

He found Stafon and Talbot getting ready for the goat chase. Neither of them was very good at the event. It required keeping a goatskin full of water away from twenty other contenders while making your way across a field of obstacles. The winner is always the biggest, strongest, brute that doesn't mind a black eye or two. Neither of them was really of that mindset but it was expected of men their age to participate.

"How about begging off and joining me while I talk to Molar?"

Stafon dropped the girding he was about to wrap himself with. "I'm not sure that's any safer."

Talbot gestured their forfeiture to the game organizer. "I talked with Bishain about the scroll. He didn't have much to say. He thinks your dad is right about the Keeper, but wasn't sure who or when."

Stafon straightened his robe. "Faith."

Tangar smirked at his response. "Right now I'm concerned with more worldly things. I want to get rid of Molar's supply of rose-blood. That way he can't tempt Tarann and I have a feeling that it'll make him less – belligerent."

Talbot scoffed. "I don't think so. I've noticed he uses a bit of it himself lately. If anything, it'll set him on a rampage looking for more."

The trio made their way to the elder's lodge and navigated the maze of cubicles situated around the spacious interior. Varying levels of opulence personalized each alcove and bore some traces of tribal heritage.

The closed curtains of Molar's room declared his non-receptive mood while Lambert reclined in his usual inebriated state next to Maron on a couch just outside.

Tangar assessed the situation. "I'll keep Lambert busy while you two sneak in and get all of the rose-blood you can find. Don't bother with anything else, just grab what you can and get out of there."

Quietly moving Lambert's spear to the floor, Tangar kicked it under the couch. "Lambert old buddy, how's it going?"

Lambert's groggily dumped Maron off the couch and staggered to his feet. "Wut... You – you needta gt outa here."

Tangar put his arm around Lambert's shoulder to shield his cohorts from view as they slipped into the private cubicle. "Well, see I need to talk to your boss for a couple of minutes. It won't take long. I'll just slip in and have a couple of words." He made as if he was going to open the curtain.

Lambert regained enough composure to grab Tangar by the arm. "No you don't. Get out of here before I kick your ass."

"Now is that any way to talk to an old friend. We should get together sometime and have a drink or something. You can bring a – friend." He watched Maron straighten her dress.

Lambert spun quickly grabbing for his spear but discovered it missing. "What have you done with my spear?"

"Spear? I don't know what you mean. I'm just here to talk to Molar."

Lambert shoved Maron aside and scrambled, throwing pillows and blankets in all directions. When, at last, he dove to look under the couch, Tangar moved to stand just behind him, blocking his ability to get off his knees. As he fumbled and bumped trying to pull the weapon free, Tangar managed to stumble and step on the shaft trapping it against the floor.

"Get out of my way!" He shoved him aside and drew the spear out.

Talbot joined the fray as if just arriving on the scene. "What's going on here? We can't have fighting in the sleeping area."

Stafon tucked a package into his shirt and slipped behind the curtain to come out at the rear of the scuffle. "Now see here. You people need to take this outside."

Lambert assessed the trio, looked quickly to see if Molar was awake, and spoke in a muffled tone. "Get out! Right now or I'm going to put this lance right through you."

Tangar straightened his robes and tried to appear unruffled. "Alright, I'll leave. Tell your boss I look forward to talking with him when he sobers up."

The trio went discreetly to the elder's meeting hall trying to be sure none of the enlightened-few observed their presence. Thoma was alone in his corner muttering to himself and moving icons on his prayer circles. "Hey Pop, how's it going?"

Scanning the room for any undue attention, he moved a new icon onto the field of play. "Well enough. What brings you to my counsel?"

Tangar leaned in close. "Do you have any use for a bunch of roses?"

Thoma's eyes narrowed as he considered his words and moved the icon deliberately into the lower arc of the diagram. "Can any hold the temptation of Vau's final embrace? The scent of the rose whispers on the untamed wind."

Stafon moved uncomfortably close, clutching the package to his waist. "Ah, I need to get back to the wife."

Tangar nodded to his father. "I'll be seeing ya later. Come on guys, let's get out of here."

As they rounded a secluded corner, Stafon cautiously handed the package to Tangar. "Good riddance. I don't want to know what you're going to do with it."

Talbot smirked at his friend's apprehension and nodded farewell to the pair. "Smart man... I don't want to know either."

Tangar stuffed the package into his shirt and started home. Hesitating at his door, he watched Tarann diligently working on a new basket. She glanced up at him for a moment, tossed her hair aside, and twisted forcefully on a stubborn spoke. Her hands clinched tightly in exasperation as she dropped the basket onto her lap. "Well, what do you want?"

"Nothing, I just wanted to see how you're doing."

"I'm doing fine. Leave me alone!" She picked up the basket and considered throwing it at him, but decided instead to take a sip of her tea. The cup sat warming near the fire and had obviously become part of her work routine.

He smiled at her resolve and stepped back out into the sun. Considering the pouch held tightly against his stomach, he searched his mind for resolution. His father's words rang in his ears. "The scent of the rose whispers on the wind." *Am I to find wisdom in that? Is there some hidden meaning I'm to find? I'm tired of his games and limericks. Perhaps he is too. Perhaps I make too much of it. His training as Seer always speaks of spirit herbs in cryptic verse to protect the ignorant.*

Making his way quickly to the cliff overlooking the bay, he gazed at the golden orb of Hea's might and called out at the top of his lungs. "Hail YodHeaVau!"

Nothing else would come.

He had set in his mind that he would offer the contraband to the gods but now it seemed too arrogant. He pulled the pouch from its hiding place and weighed its value. *To Molar it's a priceless treasure but to me it's worse than rubbish. I'm not sure there is a God to offer it to and, even if there is, why would He want it? What if I offend the gods with this wicked filth? No. It's wicked only in the hands of someone like Molar. In the right hands, it's an important part in the healing art. It can't offend God. It is a precious gift from Vau. Can I be wise enough to use it correctly?*

The vision of Tarann sitting by the hearth working her baskets and sipping her kasis tea came to him. *She faces her burden bravely. She wants so badly to be a mother that she will even suffer the imperfect treatment offered by my father. Maybe he's right. Maybe we are to each play some small part in the world to come, and it's necessary for her to know the healing of kasis for the sake of our daughter. Maybe Yod has made these plans for us. For her sake, I pray that it's true. I must have faith that it is so! I can think of no other way to go on.*

Putting the wind at his back, he opened the package and spilled the dusty brown contents. At first, it tumbled down the cliff face in clumps, but as the wind caught hold, it dispersed into finer and finer streamers that vanished completely before getting to the waves below. "Hail YodHeaVau. I return Your bounty unblemished. Please Vau, free Tarann from Your grip."

A gust of wind tugged at the pouch still dangling from his grasp. He puzzled over it for a moment. *I can cast it into the bay or bury it along the trail to hide my involvement, but no, this isn't an act of deceit. It's my declaration of defiance; my commitment to faith. The people must know what Molar has done, and what I have done to combat it.*

Folding the bag neatly into a small square, he stuffed it into his pocket and bid farewell to the evening breeze.

Tangar grabbed his weapons to get ready for a chance encounter with Lambert. "Chilc, I want you to stay close to Mom today. I have something I need to take care of and I don't want Molar coming near her."

"What? I can't. My team's in the finals."

"I'm sorry, but this is important. I wouldn't ask if it wasn't."

"Aw – come on. You really know how to ruin things."

"Yeah, that's me alright. Look, I'll make it up to you. I'll stand watch for you or something. It's just really important that Mom isn't alone. OK?"

"Yeah, OK, but you owe me. What am I supposed to tell her? She'll want to know why I'm hanging around."

"Hmm, yes... Tell her you don't feel good. Show her your bruises. Let her mother you. That should be fun."

"You have a real sick sense of fun."

"It'll be fun for her. That's what's important."

"And what are you going to be doing? Why don't you stay with her?"

He hefted his spear. "I have to go talk with some people and it may get messy. I don't want you guys involved."

"I should come with you then."

"No, you already know how to fight. You need to learn to – heal."

"You're starting to sound like the old man."

***

Talbot greeted him as he approached the high-elders court. "How did it go?"

"Nothing to it." He pulled the neatly folded envelope from his pocket and displayed it. "Now, I just need to convince Bishain that the time has come for me to take over as Seer of the lakeshore clan."

"Yeah, about that... I'm afraid he's going to want a little more convincing than your tiff with Molar."

"It's more than a tiff. I'm trying to stop him from killing people in the name of enlightenment."

"Don't tell me, tell him." He gestured to Bishain attending court.

"Hmm, yes. I think I'll wait for a private moment."

"He's not taking personal meetings today. You'll have to try again tomorrow."

"Ah – can you put in a word for me? I mean, what I have to say is kind of private."

"I'm afraid that would compromise my standing. I'm sorry, but since Nolan turned on him, he's testing my loyalty. I have to stick to the rules he's laid down or he'll replace me."

"I'm not asking for you to do anything against the rules. I just need a moment alone with him."

"All I can do is tell him you want to talk. No guarantee he'll even see you."

"Sure, understood. Tell him it's about the scrolls."

Talbot grimaced at the prospect but after ushering the next attendee into the court, he caught Bishain's ear and gestured to Tangar.

Dismissing him with a quick flick of his wrist, Bishain resumed his political deliberations.

The next two petitioners were quickly dealt with and it was finally Tangar's turn. He propped his spear at the door, submissively approached the high-elder, and began the standard formal plea. "Master, please hear my appeal..."

"Enough of that, what do you want?"

Tangar turned to see who was within earshot and was surprised to note that Talbot had dismissed the remaining petitioners. "I've come to ask that you remove Molar as Seer of the lakeshore tribe and instate me in my rightful position."

"Your plea weakens your claim. There is no right of succession. The Seer must ascend by the will of the people. You know these things. Why do you come to me thus?"

"You appointed Molar when Dad was – relieved. I just figured you needed to be involved in replacing him."

"And what does your father say about that?"

Thoma's admonishment to "take the robes" rang in his ears. He wasn't sure why he felt it necessary to keep up the ruse, but as he glanced around the room at the drapes and tapestries adorning the various alcoves and doorways, he felt uneasy about court security. "You know him. He doesn't make much sense these days."

Bishain noted his caution with approval. "His wisdom remains despite his limitations."

"Yeah, I know... So, you're not going to help me?"

"I'll follow the people's wishes."

A commotion in the outer chamber drew their attention as Molar pushed past Talbot. "Where is he?"

Lambert was still arguing about his spear when Molar burst into the room and accosted Tangar. "You thief! Where is it?"

"What? What are you talking about?"

"Don't give me that. You stole my herb. Where is it?"

A large gathering of town's folk followed the commotion and crowded the high-elder's court. Talbot was unable to restrain them to the outer chamber as they poured into the formal courtyard.

Bishain cracked the butt of his staff on the pavement several times. "Order! I'll not allow chaos. Order!"

When, at last, the crowd settled down, he returned to his throne. "Molar, state your case but I'll not tolerate blatant accusations."

"This thief stole my herbs..."

"Silence! I'll not warn you again. Tangar perhaps you can enlighten us."

Tangar considered his objectives. "Molar poisoned my wife with his herbs and caused her to lose our baby."

Bishain cracked his staff again. "I'll not listen to your unfounded allegations either. If neither of you can speak plainly, this meeting is over."

Molar straightened his untidy robes and stood erect. "Sir, if you please… This man and two of his friends forced their way into my quarters while I was resting and stole a package of highly prized medicinal herb that is critical to the treatment of several of my patients. I demand he return it immediately."

"Do you have any proof of this?"

"Lambert saw them. He was there and tried to stop them."

"Lambert? He's your 'guardian' isn't he? His testimony is of little weight in this matter. If you have no other proof, this matter is closed."

Tangar stepped forward and threw the empty packet at Bishain's feet. "Here is the pouch that once held his herb. I took it and I disposed of it."

Molar's eyes flared. "What do you mean you disposed of it? Where is it?"

"Vau's treasure was a humble offering to Hea to consummate their joining."

"You're as delusional as your father. Speak plainly. Don't drag God's name into your treachery. What did you do with it?"

"Hail YodHeaVau. Look around, the offering pleased Him. He was happy to accept Vau's treasure as I scattered it on the wind. He honors the offering with fair weather and calm seas."

"You fool. Don't you realize what you've done? That was my entire year's supply. It's a special herb that's found only in the highlands of autumn. Now I'll be without for nearly a year."

"I know exactly what it was. I'm the one who harvested it. It was the blood of the rose. It killed my son and made a slave of my wife. This herb should be used only in dire circumstances, not as a cure for a common headache. A wise Seer would know that. A wise Seer would never drink its tea for pleasure."

"You know nothing of being a Seer. You spout dogma of dead gods, steal the rightful property of the true Seer, and expect to go unpunished. Justice will be served... I demand a tribunal of the enlightened. They know the value of the medicine you have wasted. They'll judge you severely for the blasphemy you preach. They'll put an end to your delusions of being the Seer. Just like our father, they'll put you in your place."

Bishain struck his staff on the floor three times. "That's enough. I've heard all I need. Tangar, you confess to taking the herb and must pay restitution. Molar, if what Tangar has said is true, you face a far more serious judgment. You'll have your tribunal at the bonding ceremony. Now, both of you get out. I don't want to see or hear from either of you until then."

Tangar went immediately to warn Stafon. "I told them the truth. I left your name out of it, but Molar included you, so don't be surprised when they pull you in for questioning."

"What's to question? If you confessed, what can I add to that?"

"I don't know. I wouldn't put anything past him. The more people he can involve, the more likely he is to confuse things and convince them that something happened that didn't really happen."

"What about Tal?"

"He'll be alright, he was there."

"So what's next? What're you going to do?"

"I don't know. I mean, what's a 'tribunal' anyway? How do I get ready for that?"

"Take a spear."

"Yeah, I don't think that'll happen. Maybe Pop will know what to do."

"Yeah, I don't think that'll happen either. What's more important to you, winning the robes, or proving Molar's corrupt?"

"They're one and the same."

"Not even close. To win the robes you have to prove to the people that you're a better Seer than he is. To prove he's corrupt you just need to let him talk. People see through him, they're just afraid of him. They don't want to get on his bad side, lest he poison their family or refuse to treat their ailments."

"Would a good Seer do that?"

"Perhaps not, but you have to convince the whole tribe, not that he does these things, but that you would never do them."

"Is there anything in the scrolls that would help? I mean, we've spent a lot of time on them, and so far they've just been a bunch of trouble for me."

"There's the question for your dad. He sees things in them that no one else sees. Maybe he can pull something out that'll mystify people, if nothing else. I mean, it could add a spiritual aura that might win you a few votes."

"That's pretty risky. I mean, he's more likely to convince people that he's a lunatic that I shouldn't listen to."

"Well, it's something to consider if things go bad for you. What's Tal got to say about it?"

"He doesn't think he should get involved. He's still acting as Bishain's Number One. He's afraid that if he gets anymore involved, he'll lose his favor."

"Too bad... He knows the scrolls better than I do. He might be able to think of something... Just stay on the positive side. People don't like to think they've been duped."

"That's going to be hard to do. How do I stay positive when everything Molar does is wrongheaded? He nearly killed Barb, and what he's done to Tarann is depraved."

"Just the same, he'll claim your ignorance is to blame, that he did the right thing, and you messed it up."

"I know. It's hard to dispute. Maybe the better route is to appeal to everyone's sense of tribal loyalty. I mean, Molar isn't really part of the lakeshore clan. He should go back to the eastern harbor where he belongs."

"That's a hard sell too. That's why he married Maron."

"Yeah, but marriage isn't really clan membership."

"Careful there… There are others that claim kinship through marriage."

"Sure, but everyone knows it's not as strong."

"Still, it's not likely to win many votes."

"Maybe that's the key... Maybe I can convince Bishain to count only the votes of the lakeshore people. We're the only ones effected. The other villages shouldn't care, so they shouldn't get a vote."

"The enlightened from all the villages will support Molar no matter what. They'll want a vote."

"All the more reason to not allow them... I wonder if Tal could put in a good word with Bishain."

"What about the eastern village? They'll be effected if Molar's sent home."

"I just have to convince them that it's a good idea for them to get him back. I mean, what village wouldn't want two shamans to tend to their needs?"

"I don't know. They already know him for what he is and probably don't want him back."

"Yeah, true enough. I'll see if Tarann has any ideas. In the meantime, watch your back. Molar will probably sic Lambert on you to see if threats work."

As Tangar entered his hut, Tarann sat resentfully silently at the hearth twisting strands of straw into basket webbing. Chilcoat sat across from her absentmindedly stabbing his knife into a twist of straw he had bound together. Little flecks of grass rained down into a pile near his foot. Thoma sat in the far corner muttering to his talking stick as he whittled on it.

"I'm glad you're all here. I'm trying to figure out how to unseat Molar. Anyone got any good ideas, let me know."

Chilcoat scraped the pile of shavings up and tossed them into the fire. A shower of sparks danced around the column of smoke and raced out the chimney vent. "Take him hunting. He'll fall off a cliff in no time."

A vision of Chilbain formed around the boy and swept up the chimney with the sparks. Tangar warmly remembered the times he had sat around the fire with him. He would prod the embers and rhythmically chant the hunter's prayer as the sparks rose to the heavens.

"Hmm – I'd like to keep violence out of it for now. I was thinking more along the lines of arguing tribal loyalty. You know, 'he's not really part of the tribe and doesn't deserve to be their Seer'."

Tarann twisted a bundle of fiber strands into twine around her fingers. "No one **deserves** to be Seer. It's a curse that ruins good men. Look at your father. Did he deserve to be poisoned?"

Everyone looked to Thoma to see if he would respond. He blew shavings from the wand he was working and looked placidly across the room. "Tea strengthens the spirit."

Tarann dropped her shoulders, put her work aside, and began brewing a pot of tea for the old man. She set a cup of water aside for her special brew and conducted a small ritual to purify the offering. Chilcoat added a large dollop of honey, Tangar savored the refreshing tartness, and Thoma pinched a small bit of cinnamon into his cup.

"So Pop, you got any ideas on how to approach this tribunal?"

He sipped at his tea loudly. "A true Seer sees what others cannot." Placing his cup aside, he resumed his whittling and blew a bit of dust out of a delicate niche.

Tarann sipped slowly on the bitter dregs in her cup. "I hope you know what he's talking about because I don't have anything better than that. I just want to see him dead."

He looked skeptically at his father. "Hmm, yes, he certainly can be – vague when he wants to be. I guess I'm on my own."

The next few days were filled with the final rounds of various athletic events leading up to the bonding ceremony. The excitement built as the youngsters drew up their courage to take part in the ritual.

For Tangar it took the form of anxiety and foreboding. The hatred in his gut twisted Tarann's desired to see Molar dead with his father's challenge to see "what others cannot." His mind reeled, jumping from long standing dogma and cryptic verses in the scrolls to outright assassination. *Am I so weak that I can think only of divine intervention and mayhem? Surely, I can do something without dragging God into it.*

It suddenly occurred to him that to exclude God **was** the new way. *I shouldn't exclude God from this decision. It's not a weakness, it's a strength to recognize that I **can't** exclude God. I can refuse to recognize His part, but I can't exclude Him. I am a small part of Him and can't be otherwise.*

The words "I am" echoed in his thoughts. They had always just been another trifle left lingering by the old ways. They were the nonsensical claim made when playing the game of fools. They simply meant, "My turn is done, I am satisfied with the move I've made." Now he realized that it meant so much more. *It's a critical part of the prayer. It is the recognition that, if I am to be Seer, I can't be other than a small part of God. All that I do, all that I am, I do for Him.*

He gazed at the remnant of the prayer circles he had scratched into the floor days before. He couldn't help but smile as he noted that one foot stood in the circle of Yod and the other in the circle of Vau. He whispered so that none but God could hear. "Hail YodHeaVau. I am."

He, at last, dressed in his finest robes and marched defiantly across the village commons to the elder's meetinghouse. He called out over the usual crowd of courtiers gathered in the foyer. "Thoma, Seer of the lakeshore clan, I come to claim your robes."

The crowd fell silent. The formal "challenge of succession" was a nearly forgotten ritual of the old ways. The crowd slowly came to life and began grumbling. Some were scandalized that Tangar would have the audacity to invoke the old ways while others were pleased to see the show of bravado.

Stanton dispatched Lambert to fetch Molar and turned to Tangar. "Just like your father, you're a little confused. Thoma isn't the Seer of the lakeshore clan, Molar is."

His followers jeered approval of his barb.

"Molar is a pretender, appointed only to fill-in until Thoma recovers. Thoma remains the rightful Seer of the tribe."

"Thoma is a fool that doesn't even know where he is, much less how to perform the duties of Seer."

"He knows the wisdom of our tribe far better than you or Molar can ever hope to. Even under the influence of your poison, he sees things far clearer than you and your enlightened-few. He knows the wisdom of the sacred scrolls and the importance of hearing them all, not just some select verses patched together to support your corrupt schemes."

"Scrolls of outdated nonsense and dead gods have no place in an enlightened world. Your father sees things in those old rags that no one else sees. His unfortunate incident of brewing himself bad tea has tainted his vision and he imagines things that aren't real. I know, as a good son, you feel you must defend him, but the council has spoken on this issue. The scrolls of birth and death serve us well. No others are needed."

The crowd of enlightened followers jeered support and elbowed their way closer to the pair.

Thoma emerged from the meetinghouse on Caran's arm. He wore his ceremonial robes and carried his talking stick as if it were a scepter. "Who claims my robes?"

The formal response brought everyone's attention back to Tangar.

Stanton grimaced as Lambert returned with his spear in one hand and Molar clinging unsteadily to the other. The pair navigated to the front of the crowd while Molar held his free hand up to shelter his eyes from the midmorning glare. He staggered as Lambert nudged his haggard frame forward. His clothes looked as if he had slept in them and he seemed unable to focus on what was happening.

Tangar smirked, knowing the signs of the craving all too well. "Ah, the provisional Seer of the lakeshore clan has arrived. Tell me oh wise one – what is the enlightened view of not having your morning tea? What will you give me for a whiff of rose blossoms?"

Molar squinted at him trying to focus. "You're a thief and a fool. My people will take care of you and your family."

"You threaten me? I hereby invoke a tribunal of the high council to deal with your blatant threats to women and children."

Molar, at last, seemed to grasp the situation. "I've already called for a tribunal."

"You mean, you've asked if you or I should be considered Seer of the lakeshore clan?"

"Don't play dumb with me. You know what we're talking about. You claim to be the rightful holder to the Seer's robes and everyone knows that I'm the Seer of the lakeshore clan."

"Then, you recognize this is a concern of the lake people, not a federated tribunal?"

"What? No. That's not what I said. I said, everyone should hear what an incompetent fool and thief you are so they understand why I'm their Seer."

Bishain and his entourage pushed their way through the crowd. He struck his staff three times on the first step. "I told you that I will not stand for this disorder. The court will assemble at the bonding and not until then."

Tangar bowed courteously to Bishain. "Master, I mean no disrespect. I was just trying to clarify the issue. It's plain to see that this is a matter for the lakeshore clan. It need not detract from the bonding festivities of the whole tribe. The appointment of the Seer for the lakeshore doesn't concern the western clan nor even the northern clan. This issue need not go beyond **my** people."

Molar struggled to keep from staggering. "This issue goes far beyond the borders of the lake. This is a matter of correcting wayward thought. These poor fools have been led astray by the delusional wanderings of his father. Everyone has seen him talking to rocks and sticks. Is that the kind of leader these people need? No. They need to be brought into the light. They need to leave the old ways behind and seek real, down-to-earth, solutions for the less fortunate, not some fanciful vision of plenty for a lucky few."

Bishain grimaced at having his hand forced. "At the bonding!" He turned from the crowd and climbed the steps into the meetinghouse.

Tangar tossed down the stolen herb pouch. "Here, here is your remedy. It's plain to see that the blood of the rose calls to you. I can see in your eyes that you can think of nothing else. Go ahead take it. Show everyone the enlightenment you offer them. Show them how you bow down to Vau's sweet call of pleasure, of forgetfulness, of death."

Molar's eyes widened at the sight. "Let the people see this... You stole this medicine from me. I'll take it, not because I crave it, but because it is rightfully mine. I need it to treat **my** people."

As he bent to retrieve the pouch, Tangar put his foot on it. "Not so fast. I'm not sure this is the same stuff I took. You know how incompetent I am. I might have gotten it mixed up with some banton root. You wouldn't want that to happen would you?"

Several of the crowd snickered at the thought of Molar and the laxative spending the night together. Stanton assessed the shifting mood of the audience and leaned to whisper to his second in command.

Molar yanked the edge of the pouch from under his foot. "You don't need to worry about that."

"Oh, but I do worry. You see, that's my job as Seer. I worry that perhaps I've given you the wrong herb, or perhaps I've given you too much and you'll become dependent on it, or not enough, and you'll suffer needlessly. I worry that something as small as a thorn prick, when not treated correctly, will result in the loss of a foot, or worse, the loss of a life. A real Seer worries about these things. So, you be careful with that."

Molar's hand quaked visibly as he clinched the herb pouch. "You just stay out of my way. I've things to do."

Stanton grimaced at the folly and dispatched one of the lesser runners to follow as Molar fled with his treasure clinched greedily to his chest.

Stafon edged up next Tangar and whispered. "I thought you got rid of that stuff."

"It's a long story. Let's just say, he's not going to be happy with his prize."

"Ah, you finally decided to poison him?"

"Not exactly, Pop gave me some Tanasin root. I figured it'll keep him busy for a while."

"Tanasin? Where'd he get Tanasin?"

"**That's** the long story. I'll tell you about it some day. In the meantime, I need to get Pop ready for the ceremony."

"What's to get ready? He looks better than I've seen him in a long time."

"That's just it. I think maybe he should look – less normal."

"That shouldn't be much of a problem. Just muss up his hair. That bush looks crazy enough when it's combed."

"Hmm, yes, that gives me an idea. I'll see you at the ceremony."

As the sun set, Bishain stood on the upper gallery above the temple entrance and held his scepter to the sky. "Hail YodHeaVau. We gather in Your name to bond anew."

With that formality out of the way, the women started to chant the call to blending. The flirtatious assembly of young women soon disappeared into the temple, followed by the somewhat disorderly gathering of young men.

Tangar's anxiety grew as he guided his father along the path leading into the temple grounds. The crowd had already started into the courtyard and stopped as the pair passed. Thoma wore his most elaborate ceremonial robes and carried a staff adorned with colorful streamers of cloth. They had both shaved their heads and painted the opposite sides of their faces bright red.

As the pair made their way to the base of the elder's mound, all eyes were upon them. Bishain sat in regal splendor on his throne at the topmost peak of the platform. He had an unmistakable smirk on his face as he called the meeting to order. "Before we get started with the bonding ceremony we have some business to conduct. A claim has been made for the Seer's robes of the lakeshore clan. I ask all of the interested parties to approach."

Tangar pulled the hood back on his robe, accentuating his shaved head, and strode confidently to the base of the elder's platform. "I claim the Seer's robes of the lakeshore clan."

Bishain again smirked at the sight of the novice shaman trained in the old ways. "Does anyone contest this claim?"

The crowd grumbled in confusion until Lambert called out. "Here, Molar's the rightful Seer."

Molar staggered along the path clutching Lamberts arm for support. "Thas right. Mm th Ser."

Bishain looked in obvious disdain at Molar and turned to Thoma. "Is there anyone else?"

Thoma drew his staff up and struck it hard on the stones. "I hold the Seer's robes and I will not yield them to the unworthy."

The crowd mumbled in surprise that Thoma was coherent. He not only looked the part, he spoke clearly and without hesitation.

Tangar nodded at the correct formal response to his challenge. "I am trained in the ways of our forefather's. I know the wisdom of the sacred scrolls and I ask my people if any have ever been mistreated by me?"

Molar's hunched figure gazed listlessly from side-to-side as if he was trying to figure out where he was. "I cn atest that you nrly killd tha girl wit yr botchd wrk."

Lambert quickly agreed. "That's right. The Blain girl almost died because of him. Molar here had to cut her foot off to save her life. You can ask anyone."

The followers of the new way jeered approval.

Tangar clinched his fist. "That's a good idea. Let's ask Barb herself what happened."

Bishain cracked his staff on the platform and looked quickly to Talbot standing nearby with Barb. "That won't be necessary. I'm sure she's been through enough without you dragging her through it all again. Let's concentrate on more pressing issues. What of the theft of Molar's herb?"

Tangar stiffened at the rebuke. "I – I took the herb from Molar while he slept. I admit that, and I'd do it again."

Molar's supporters jeered and shouted disgust.

Bishain cracked his staff again. "That will be enough of that. If you are not a party to this dispute, you have no say in the matter. If you insist on interrupting, I'll ask you to leave. Now, Tangar, how do you propose to compensate Molar for the herb?"

"Master, the herb I took was the 'Blood of the Rose'. He is captive to its magic. He no longer sees right or wrong. He hears only the whisper of forgetfulness of the rose. It's common knowledge that it serves only to sedate in the direst of circumstances and should not be used lightly. No true shaman would use the herb for a simple stomach pain, especially for a pregnant woman. This is clear proof that Molar either doesn't know what he's doing or doesn't care for the people he serves. In either case, he shouldn't be Seer."

Bishain cracked his staff again. "I didn't hear anything in all of that on how you intend to compensate Molar for his loss."

The crowd again jeered agreement.

Bishain stood and swept his staff across the crowd. "I warned you people. Now, get out! You heard me, get out."

The crowd grumbled and complained as the temple guards ushered them out of the plaza.

Bishain returned to his throne and sat arranging his robes to cascade down the platform. "Now, speak. How are you going to compensate for your theft of the sacred herb?"

Tangar considered his continued apprenticeship under Molar. "I – I have given him the herb he needs to face the craving of the rose. For he, himself, abuses the herb for his own pleasure. This is not the wisdom of a Seer. This is the action of a weak man relying on drugs to soothe his conscience while he lets outsiders control his every move. I'll not allow my people to fall into such a trap of deception."

Bishain turned to Molar's glazed expression. "What have you to say to this reparation?"

Molar seemed to not understand what was being asked. His eyes wandered about the room dwelling on flames and flags that flickered in the breeze.

Bishain turned to Tangar. "You say you deny him the rose, but what have you given him?"

Tangar looked timidly at his feet. "I gave him kasis to dull the craving."

Bishain gestured at Molar's apparent loss of concern. "This is not the glow of kasis."

"Ah, yeah, I sort of mixed in a little tanasin to make it look more like rose-blood."

Bishain glanced quickly at Thoma and returned to glare at Tangar whispering. "Where did you get tanasin?"

Tangar looked to his father, pulled his hood on to shield his face, and lowered his voice. "Just as in the sacred scrolls, I followed the wisdom guide to the sky-temple and walked with the spirits of the Shanare. They whispered of times past, of wise people, and old ways. They said that Molar's affliction cannot be cured. He must desire the pain of life itself more than the bliss of the rose. For him to gain such knowledge he must first know their spirits through the wisdom of the 'little man'."

Bishain looked questioningly to Thoma, pulled his hood on, and leaned in close to Tangar. "The spirits of the sky-temple speak to few. I warn you, this knowledge is guarded highly and should not be spoken of again."

Straitening to address Lambert, Bishain spoke clearly. "I can't deal with one so – confused. Take him away until he sobers up. And see if you can clean him up."

As Lambert hauled his ward away, Bishain turned to Tangar. "You're dealing with things that go far beyond your appointment as

Seer. The enlightened-few will not stand for their chosen-one being treated in this way.”

“I know of no other way to rid my people of such wrongful thinking. You’ve tasked me with knowing the forgotten scrolls, and I find in them many puzzles of times long forgotten, and a future that whispers of much hardship. They speak of children that find strength in the old ways. I know of no way to teach these children than to turn them away from Molar’s enlightened path. If I’m reading them wrong, please tell me so that I may know the truth.”

“The ways of the enlightened-few reach far beyond Molar. They promise days of plenty without want or strife if only everyone will work together for the betterment of all. These are hard beliefs to combat with old stories of troubles and hardship. No one wants to hear that their path is leading to toil and suffering.”

“You know as well as I that the ‘few’ don’t really believe in their new ways. They simply use them to control people into following their decree. They have no respect for people that work hard. The only thing they believe in is their own cleverness in not working as their underlings do. They believe they need to think for the poor fools that do their bidding. They believe that if the people are dumb enough to listen to them, they deserve no more than to serve their overlords.”

“This is what you see in the forgotten scrolls?”

“This is what I see in the enlightened-few, scrolls or no scrolls.”

The bonding ceremony took place with little departure from traditional norms. Some youngsters went away disappointed either that they weren't seen fit for pairing or that the right mate didn't step forward.

One of those was Caran. She was included in the youngest group of women and, thus, wasn't expected to actually bond with anyone. Nonetheless, she was disappointed that no one stepped forward to seek her hand. She blamed it on her stout frame and serious nature but it was more likely her cherubic features that frightened would-be suitors.

Chilcoat sensed her disappointment and wanted to comfort her but he was too young to participate. *It's not right for her to feel bad over something so silly. The council would never let her bond this year anyway, so it just seems hurtful to have her join in the ceremony.*

He rushed to grab her as she came down the women's knoll but she wasn't open to his overture and wanted only to weep on her Charona's shoulder.

The consummation ritual was about to get started so everyone, not directly involved, was ushered out of the courtyard. As the entourage of elders filed out through the access tunnel, Lambert stood waiting. "Ah, hey, Molar's ready to talk now."

Talbot quickly blocked his approach to allow Bishain to pass. "Formal receptions will be entertained after the evening meal."

"He's ready now."

"He'll have to wait. Protocol must be observed."

"I'm not sure that's a good idea. He may not be willing to wait."

Bishain interrupted their bickering. "Willing or able? If he wishes to exhibit his wisdom by forcing his will on a very hungry judicial committee, so be it. Talbot, gather the interested parties in the meetinghouse, I'll be there shortly."

Thoma retained his stained face as he sat in his usual place, moving icon's around the symbol etched into the floor. Tangar arrived with Tarann at his side and attempted to gather his father into a more dignified posture. It was of no avail. He continued to assess people as they entered the chamber and select icons befitting their stature. A large cluster of rough pebbles gathered in one segment of the diagram.

Bishain finally entered along with Nolan and Talbot. The high-elder greeted friends and dignitaries as he slowly meandered toward the far end of the hall. He stopped to address Thoma. "It's beginning to look a little lopsided."

Thoma smiled in greeting and moved a colorful twig into a small cluster of objects in the third segment of the diagram. "The enlightened support their cause."

Bishain tipped his head toward the stage. "And so, the time has come. Join me now."

Thoma looked skeptically at Nolan, adjusted one the icons across the diagram, and rose to take his staff firmly in hand. "The clan speaks clearly."

Bishain moved slowly to the chair that had been set up at the far end of the room on a raised platform. He stood behind it with his hands on the backrest and bowed his head thoughtfully. "We come together to mourn the passing of a noble man and great Seer. His robes pass to the rightful without question. Come old friend, come and sit that we may honor your memory."

He gave a nod to the women that stood by his side and they began a mournful rendition of a favored love song. The crowd stood in silent shock as Thoma stepped solemnly to stand in front of the chair. He placed his hands on top of his old friend's for several moments then turned slowly to sit.

As the song lingered on the last refrain, Bishain pulled his hood off. "This man has served without fault for many years and now must pass, as we all must. The sacred scrolls speak plainly of the burdens of birth and death, for that is our destiny. What they don't speak of clearly is the life we are to lead, for that is something each of us must discover for ourselves. Yod teaches His wisdom through this struggle. Thoma has lived a noble life of service that will be missed dearly. His last wish is that his people should know a worthy Seer to replace him. To that end, we come together now to pass the robes of the lakeshore clan. Molar step forward."

Tangar flushed with anger and was about to protest when his father gave him a stern look of reprimand.

Molar navigated boldly through the crowd. He had apparently found an alternate source of rose-blood and moved confidently amongst friends and supporters. His formal ceremonial robes flowed triumphantly about him in flashes of sunrise gold and crimson.

Bishain looked dismayed as Molar swaggered to stand in front of the crowd. "You don't wear the robes of the lakeshore clan."

"What? No. These are my robes from the eastern harbor, when I was first ordained Seer. I figured it was fitting, and besides, they're more – colorful don't you think?"

"No. You don't understand. You are not to wear the robes of the lakeshore clan. You may leave now."

"What? Now wait a minute. Who said I'm not to wear the robes? I don't remember voting on it."

"I have spoken with the elders of the lakeshore clan and they have very little faith in your actions as Seer."

"What do you mean lakeshore elders? We need the whole tribe to vote on something this important."

"The import of their Seer lies wholly in the hands of the lakeshore clan. You were assigned Seer duties only so long as Thoma was unable to fulfill the function. And, as you can see, he is fully capable now, so you are no longer needed."

"What? He's – he's not capable of doing anything except talking to rocks." He gestured at the prayer circles etched in the floor. "Just look at that mess he's made. These are not the acts of a capable Seer."

Tangar unclenched his fist and pointed to the cluster of stones in the circles. "These are not just any stones he talks to. See this one with the deep flaw through its center. This is you Molar. These are the circles of life described in the sacred scrolls. This is the wisdom of the old ways. He has placed you here along with all of your friends of the enlightenment." He nudged the pile of pebbles with his toe.

"If you knew the scrolls as he does, you'd know that he has placed you in the arms of Hea, the pitiless god of lifeless things. This is a place of great power, but it is a cold unfeeling power without morals. That is what your new ways of enlightenment teach. Power without beliefs, without compassion, without concern for the people you owe for your existence."

Molar scoffed and kicked at the collection of stones. "I'll take the power of enlightenment over this nonsense any day. I have plenty of compassion for my people. Just ask any of them. I give them the care they need without all this mumbo-jumbo."

"You take food from their tables, clothes off their backs, and steal their spirits with your drugs. These are not the acts of compassion. These are the acts of a greedy man, hungry for the power that mindless slaves provide."

Thoma rose from his chair and cracked the butt of his staff on the floor. "I've heard enough. My mission of learning of the inner workings of the enlightenment is done. Little wisdom can come from such a shallow understanding of life. The new ways are easy for any to understand and follow; too easy. The select few ask only that their followers blindly submit devotional offerings and in return, they dole out a meager subsistence wrapped in mind numbing platitudes and herbs of obedience. I'll not allow the lakeshore clan to fall prey to such deceit. I award my robes to Tangar. May he not regret this challenge."

It took several moments for the crowd to recognize what had happened. At first they mumbled and conferred, then began shouting in support of their particular faction.

Thoma handed his staff to Tangar, shrugged his robes from his shoulders, and handed them to him. "My robes are yours, but with them comes much pain. For that, I'm sorry. The willful ignorance of men challenges the truth known only to YodHeaVau. Seek His council in all that you do."

With Stanton's encouragement, Molar grabbed at Bishain's sleeve. "Now wait a minute. You can't just disregard the wishes of the entire tribe like that. I demand a full tribunal."

Talbot stepped in and removed Molar's hand with a quick flick of his wrist. "Your time has passed. The people involved have spoken. None of the other tribes want to relinquish their sovereignty to a federated tribunal, for that's what you are asking. Go now. Find a tribe that will accept your – talents."

Molar's eyes flared. "I'll not be talked to by a novice in this way. Bishain, get your puppy out of my sight."

Bishain looked solemnly at the pair. Handing his staff to Talbot, he shrugged his robes from his shoulders and handed them to him. "My robes are yours, but with them comes much pain. For that, I'm sorry. The willful ignorance of men challenges the truth known only to YodHeaVau. Seek His council in all that you do."

He turned and walked away leaving the bewildered crowd. Talbot silently watched his beloved mentor put his arm around Thoma as the pair left the room talking quietly to one another.

A dazed Talbot turned to Tangar who looked equally confused. Stafon approached dressed in the ceremonial robes of the western clan. "Welcome to the club boys. We have things to do, so if you're done standing around, let's get to it."

The small amount of herb Molar had negotiated for the ceremony was wearing off and he looked ill. His breathing was heavy and sweat ran down his face. The craving gnawed at his gut and he could think of nothing but where he could get more. For he knew that, while the shaman of each tribe usually held a small quantity of rose-blood for medicinal purposes, none of them was likely to dispense it for his enjoyment. There would be no more until next autumn's harvest and now that Tangar is the Seer of the lakeshore clan, the harvest would be his to dispense.

He turned to Stanton for support but found only his back as he ushered his entourage of the enlightened out of the hall following Bishain. They laughed and jostled each other in good-natured ribbing as if nothing had happened. A flush of nausea swept over Molar as he turned to Tangar. "Let's get a few things straight. I'll stay on for a while, until you get used to things. You know? I'll help you get settled in."

Tangar pulled his robes on. "That won't be necessary. I think I can handle it."

Tarann ran up and put her arms around Tangar. "Wow, that's not what I expected." The pair embraced shamelessly for several moments.

Molar tugged fitfully at his hair trying to rid himself of the ants crawling up the back of his neck. Lambert scoffed at his awkward appearance and pulled Maron in close under his arm. "Come on; let's go see if we can find some wine."

Tarann pulled a pouch from her belt and held it out to Molar. "Here, you look like you could use this."

He gazed, contemptuously at the pouch. "I've had enough of your poison."

She nodded knowingly. "I've said those very words myself."

The new Seers joked about the fit of various tassels and fobs dangling from their elaborate costumes. Tarann pulled on one particularly unattractive ribbon. "I suppose there's a story with this, but it doesn't add much to your image."

Tangar spun slowly with his arms outstretched. "Hmm, yes. I'll have to ask about some of this stuff."

"I don't suppose you'd let me wash it? It's kind of – ripe."

Reaching into one of the pockets, he retrieved Thoma's talking wand. It had a length of colored yarn tied carefully around it. "We'll work out something. Right now, I need to see how Dad's doing. That little ritual was kind of weird. I mean, the way they were talking, I expected him to drop dead or something."

Stafon interjected. "Kind-of-weird doesn't cover the half of it. Tal, did you know this was going to happen?"

Talbot was also exploring the various pockets and folds of his robes. "No. I mean, Bishain spoke of retiring from time-to-time, but he never mentioned when... I think all this enlightenment crap has gotten to him. That must be why he tasked us with reading the lost scrolls. I think both of those old thieves planed this whole thing a long time ago for when they figured we were ready."

Tarann noted the gift knot used to secure the yarn around the wand. "You mean those conniving old scoundrels planned all of this?"

Talbot turned to Tarann. "Well, probably not the stuff you had to go through. But, I think maybe that's what convinced them to go through with their scheme. It doesn't matter now. They'll never admit it. They'll just claim it's meant to be and point to some obscure line in one of the scrolls. You know how they are."

She playfully snatched the yarn from Tangar before he could twist it around the stick again. "Speaking of obscure – show me all that stuff about our daughter."

"Ah, well, we'll have to go ask Bishain if he'll let us look at the scrolls."

Stafon scoffed. "He's probably down at the shore fishing by now. Besides, they belong to Talbot now, right?"

Talbot flushed at the realization. "Ah, yeah, I think that's a good idea. We need to consecrate the passing of the two souls that has taken place here today. Reading the lost scrolls sounds fitting, maybe now we'll see their truth."

The three couples timidly made their way to the high-elder's inner sanctum. The elaborate wall hangings and carpets muffled their presence as if they weren't really there.

Barb stomped her wooden foot several times. "Just like back in the old days. I can finally walk quietly."

Tarann ran her hand over one of the more elaborate wall hangings. "A person could get used to this."

Tangar retrieved the ancient scrolls and pulled one from their shroud. "I think this is the one." He placed it on the table and carefully unrolled the brittle parchment. Running his fingers along the lines of text, he mumbled to himself while everyone wandered around the opulent surroundings poking at trinkets and stroking fabrics.

Talbot was familiar with the room and felt more dread than wonder. The thought of being the high-elder struck him for the first time. *What am I supposed to do with All of this – stuff?*

At last, Tangar spoke clearly. "Here, this is it. See, it says here that 'the mother of the one foretold shall walk amid the temple of the sky'."

Tarann pulled herself away from an intricate clay sculpture. "What's that got to do with anything? That doesn't tell me anything about our daughter."

"Ah, well, the mother of 'the one'. That's our daughter. The shaman witch..."

"Don't give me that. I didn't hear anything about a shaman."

"OK, wait a minute. I'll find it." Tangar went back to fingering the document while everyone resumed exploring the room.

Talbot stood silently at the throne staring at the intricate carvings. Barb approached to put her arm around his shoulder. "It'll be OK. You'll be great at it."

He gave her a timid smile. "I'm glad you think so. I'll remind you of that when twenty unhappy people are pounding on your door."

Tangar tapped repeatedly on the document and placed the talking wand under a line of text. It looked different to him. The freshly carved nighthawk symbol of the lakeshore clan stood out in unblemished importance. An ominous feeling crept into his mind as he noticed that, while his father had carved the symbol with exceptional care, it had a distinctive cut separating one of the wings from its body. *That crafty old buzzard has done it again. He can't just talk with me like a normal person, he has to hide the message in mysteries and puzzles. Well, I don't have time for your games now Dad.*

"Here, it says here, 'a witch of good fortune known to all as the Keeper of the Word and the Warrior of Truth shall be born to mark the coming of the end'."

Tarann leaned over the text. "The coming of the end. That doesn't sound very good."

"Maybe Dad can explain it better. It's all mixed up with a bunch of stuff about Hea bonding with Vau and begetting the children of Yod at the end of time. You have to read the whole thing."

"Hmm and in the meantime I'm just supposed to let you brainwash my baby."

"Well, brainwash is a little harsh. Let's just say I'll teach her what I know."

Laura nudged Tarann on the shoulder. "You're going to have to spell it out for him."

Tarann smirked at her remark and handed her packet of herbs to him. "OK... I'm going to have a baby, and I want you to keep your hands off of her for three years. Is that plain enough?"

"You're what? Sure, sure three years will be fine. God, I love you."